THE CAREY BLOOD

Thomas Carey Westerns
Book One

Irving A Greenfield

THE CAREY
BLOOD

Published by Sapere Books.

24 Trafalgar Road, Ilkley, LS29 8HH

saperebooks.com

ISBN: 978-1-80055-767-3

ONE

He leaned against the left side of the open doorway and squinted as he looked past the huge front yard, past the rough-hewn wooden fence, across the wide expanse of the dun-colored Texas plain — and even beyond the distant bluish-gray hills, to where the sky was streaked with large swathes of red, intermixed with bands of yellow and deepening violet. Though it was only the end of April, the day that was slowly dying had been as hot as any in June. But even as he stood there, watching the colors change in the western sky, the wind had come up blowing steadily out of the north and chilled the air, though not sufficiently to drive him back into the house.

He wasn't a tall man, but because of the way he stood and his barrel-like chest, he seemed larger than he was. He had broad shoulders and long, powerful arms, and in the fading light his leathery-looking face seemed several shades darker than usual. His hair and the stubble on his chin were pure white. He stood without making a movement or giving the slightest indication that in the room directly behind him was his son Thomas.

When the brilliant colors of the sunset were almost gone William Carey still remained in the open doorway, his eyes focused on the last orange-red streak that looked to him more like a tongue of flame than the combination of cloud and light. And even when this faded he remained in the doorway, looking at the dark masses of the distant hills that were almost ten miles from where he stood. Ten miles of rich grazing land that belonged to him and some day would belong to his sons, or at least to the youngest one, Thomas, if he ever settled down and started acting like a man instead of a wild kid — or, worse, a wild Indian.

The land and the cattle on it meant something to William. They had not only cost him years of toil, but each square mile had been paid for with the blood of the men — Indians and white alike — who tried to rip the land from his grasp. The land had also cost William his wife Martha, whose strength had given out after she had borne Thomas.

He shifted his eyes slightly to the right, where the flat plain suddenly rose up in a small knoll, crowned by the three scraggly cottonwood trees he had planted after he had buried Martha. His eldest son, John, had left the ranch ten years ago and was now in England. That was a price he had not expected to pay! Clem, his second son, was up north at Yale University studying law. Clem had already written that he had no intentions of coming back to the ranch. When he finished studying, he hoped to go into practice in Dallas or some other big city, with an eye to becoming a politician.

William shifted his position, resting more of his weight on his right foot than his left and moving his back against the left side of the open doorway. Everything he saw in the fast-fading light was tangible evidence that he had done something with the life the good Lord had given him. The ranch provided the measure of his own worth to himself and to other men. He had worked his whole life in order to make the Carey name mean something to other men, and had succeeded. The W Bar C brand was known throughout southwest Texas and, by the living God, William was not going to let any man — even if the man happened to be his own son — do anything that would hurt the ranch. That was why he had made special arrangements for Thomas, only William knew that as soon as he told his son what he had done, the boy would kick like a bronco and probably go running off. But William was willing to gamble that Thomas possessed some common sense, and once the boy had time to think things over he would come back and agree to marry Sam Wicker's daughter, Helen.

William took a deep breath, savoring the cool scent of the land, and then slowly exhaled. But still he did not turn to his son. A few more minutes one way or another wouldn't make much difference once he said what he had to say to the boy.

Thomas had known that something was bothering his father the moment the old man left the table without first having finished his dinner. 'Waste not, want not,' was one of the homilies his father had drummed into his head from the time he had been a small boy. In fact, the old man still used it whenever the opportunity came along.

Equally significant was where and the way his father was standing. Experience had taught Thomas that whenever his father had something on his mind, he always looked out over the open plains at sunset. It was almost as though he hoped to find the answer to whatever the problem was in the shifting shapes and colors of the clouds.

Thomas shrugged, but remained silent and continued to eat the thick juicy steak and hash brown potatoes that Maria, the housekeeper and cook, had prepared for dinner. He figured that if the matter concerned him his father would sooner or later tell him. Besides, he was more concerned with his own thoughts than trying to guess what was bothering the old man. And his own thoughts at the moment were completely centered on the coming Saturday night, when he would ride some fifteen miles to the town of Paso Diablo to see Lisa Mendoza.

Just hearing her name in his brain was more than enough to make him stop chewing, close his eyes and remember what her naked body was like the last time he lay with her. She was part white, part Mex and part Comanche. But he didn't give a damn what her bloodlines were as long as she was his woman. Even as Thomas thought about her he felt his blood begin to race.

He had been sleeping with women ever since he had been sixteen, for even at that age he had the body of a man — tall, lean, raw-boned. He had sandy brown hair and green eyes like those of a cat. The last five years had put more muscle on him and made him more loose-limbed, but otherwise he was the same.

No, that wasn't quite true. There were other changes. There was a long scar on the right side of his face that came from a knife fight, and a scar on his left arm, just below the shoulder, where he had taken a bullet in the gunfight in which he had killed his first man. And now he had a reputation for being a man with a mean temper and a fast gun.

In many ways he looked like his father: both were dark-complexioned men, but of the two Thomas' face was the less handsome. There was a pugnacious jut to his jaw and a sharpness of features that had made more than one man think twice about starting any trouble with him. And since he had taken to sporting a long full mustache turned down at the ends, the way the Mex vaqueros wore theirs, his appearance was all the more menacing.

But in spite of the way he looked — or perhaps because of it, and the fact that Lisa knew he was a man whom other men feared — she became his woman whenever he was in Paso Diablo. Thomas didn't bother too much with questioning the reasons why she shared her bed with him and gave him her body. It was enough that she did. And from the very first time he made love to her he wanted her to be his alone. The knowledge that other men used her tore at his insides, the way a buzzard rips at the guts of a dead steer. Just thinking about it made him angry. He opened his eyes and began to violently chew the piece of meat in his mouth.

Suddenly he realized that his father had turned around and was looking at him. Thomas wondered if the old man had seen him a few moments before when his eyes had been closed? Probably not. The light inside the room was too dim.

William Carey took one step into the room, stopped, and said, 'Sam Wicker came by today.'

Thomas cut another slice of steak, impaled it on a fork and popped it into his mouth without commenting about what his father had just told him.

'Sam said that if Mr Lincoln became President, there was sure to be trouble.'

'That's the talk,' Thomas commented after he'd swallowed the piece of steak. 'Some folks claim that it will mean war between the North and South.'

William nodded gravely. 'God forbid!'

'God has little truck with the politicians from either the North or the South,' Thomas said. 'And if you ask me, He doesn't seem to give a damn about the slaves either, otherwise He'd have freed them a long time ago.'

William knew that his son was baiting him, as he always did whenever the subject of God came up. Silently he asked the Almighty to forgive Thomas, and then he said aloud, 'Helen sent her regards to you.'

'Oh?' Thomas set his knife and fork down and looked up at his father. 'I haven't seen her for the better part of a year.'

'Maybe you should ride over to their place and pay her a visit,' William quickly suggested. 'Sam says she's become right womanly. How old is she now?'

'You know she's a year younger than me,' Thomas answered, beginning to sense that there was some connection between his father's behavior and Sam Wicker's visit.

'A year difference,' William said, taking another step toward the table where his son sat, 'is hardly any difference at all.'

Thomas nodded his agreement and stood up. Whatever game was afoot, he'd play it as though he was playing poker — straight-faced and close to the vest.

'There are some around here,' William commented, 'who think Helen Wicker is a mighty fetching young woman, the kind that any fellow with sense would be glad to marry. Especially since her daddy already said he'll give half his spread for her dowry.'

Thomas could feel the anger in him begin to burn, but still he managed to keep it under control. 'Some men like a palomino or a pinto; I myself don't like anything but a quarter horse.'

'What's that supposed to mean?' William asked sharply. 'I wasn't talking about horses. I was talking about a woman, Sam Wicker's daughter.'

Thomas chuckled.

'I didn't say anything funny,' William told his son.

'A man has to ride both, doesn't he?'

William stepped closer to the table. 'You don't talk about a woman that way,' he hissed. 'Helen is a lady.'

'Meaning?' Thomas questioned angrily.

'She's not like that whore you see in Paso Diablo.'

'So that's it?' Thomas exclaimed, stepping around to the front of the table so that he stood just a short distance from his father. 'Well, Helen Wicker may be a lady but she's not my idea of a good ride. And as for my whore,' he said, 'she's more woman than Helen will ever be.'

'Now listen to me, Thomas,' William said in a low but authoritative voice, 'you're going to stop seeing that woman in Paso Diablo —'

Thomas started to say something.

'You listen, I said,' William told him. 'I told Sam that you're going to marry Helen.'

'What?'

'You heard me,' William answered tightly. 'You're going to marry Helen and settle down before some man with a faster gun lays you out.'

'I can take care of myself,' Thomas growled. 'And I don't need you to find me a woman. I've already got a woman.'

'You've got a whore!' his father shouted. 'A damn half-breed bitch that will lay with any man if he has the price.'

Thomas started for his father with his hand raised to strike.

'Why not go for your gun?' William challenged, not moving an inch.

His words stopped Thomas, and he slowly lowered his hand. 'I am not going to do it,' he said. 'I have no feelings for Helen.'

'I'm not interested in your feelings,' William said. 'This ranch and half the Wickers' place will be yours. That should give you some feelings.'

Thomas shook his head. 'You don't have any right —'

'You're not of legal age yet,' William answered, 'so I guess I still have some rights.'

'But not to get me married to a woman —'

'Rather that than see you tied to that slut in Paso Diablo.'

'I love her.'

William snorted. 'You call wallowing in lust love?' he shouted. 'Why, she's just a bitch in heat and you're nothing more than a hound dog going after her.'

'I am not going to marry —'

'Either you marry Helen Wicker or you can clear out of here!' William growled. 'I'm doing what I think is best for you. Not only are you getting a good woman, but you're coming into a mighty nice piece of property, which is a helluva lot more than you deserve.'

'If you're so damn anxious to get hold of Sam's place,' Thomas yelled, 'why the hell don't *you* marry the bitch?'

Before William realized it, he was moving, and the back of his hand slammed against his son's face with such force that blood instantly streamed from the boy's nose. 'You'll marry her or you'll get out!' he said, breathing heavily.

Thomas' right hand had dropped to his gun. Had it been any other man who had struck him, he would have killed him. But he couldn't make his fingers curl around the gun. His hand trembled and fell to his side.

'Remember,' William said, realizing how far he had pushed Thomas, 'either you marry or you get out. Understand?'

Thomas drew his sleeve across the bottom of his nose and streaked it with blood.

'Do you understand?' William demanded to know.

Thomas nodded.

'I want to hear it!'

'I understand,' Thomas said. 'I understand.' He sidestepped his father and walked slowly toward the open door.

'Where are you going?' William asked, wheeling around.

Thomas stopped, looked at him and said, 'You know where.'

'You have three days to settle your business with that slut in Paso Diablo. If you're not back by then, don't bother coming back.'

Thomas said nothing. He walked out of the house and down to the stable to saddle his horse. Of all the things he might have imagined his father doing, forcing him to marry a woman he didn't love had never entered his imagination. Nor had he ever thought that his father would strike him.

One had happened, and the other would happen unless he could find a way to stop it.

When he had finished saddling Gray he led him out of the stable and swung into the saddle. A moment later he touched his spurs into the flanks of the animal. Gray reacted instantly and, bolting forward, Thomas galloped past the open door without a backward glance. He knew his father was standing there.

The old man had put the deck of cards on the table and had drawn first. So far the old man held the top card. The next three days would give Thomas a chance to draw. With some luck he might pull out an ace.

Thomas slowed Gray to an easy canter and hoped that by the time he reached Paso Diablo Lisa would be free to spend the rest of her time with him. The memory of her body filled his brain and fired his blood.

Paso Diablo was at the junction of Diablo Creek and the Nueces River. A half-dozen wooden buildings faced each other across its dusty main street. On the far end stood the courthouse, the jail, and the sheriff's office, all under one roof. There was a small Methodist church, a blacksmith, a livery stable, a general store and various other shops including the office of a transportation company that ran a weekly stage between Paso Diablo and Fort Worth. And there was the Broken Horn Saloon, where the local cowboys gathered to drink, gamble, and buy a short stint of pleasure in the arms of a woman.

Lisa worked in the Broken Horn Saloon but she lived in a small shack with Simon, her teenage brother, close to the rushing water of Diablo Creek.

It was well past midnight when Thomas reined Gray to a halt on a small rise just outside of town. The light from the April moon touched the drab wooden buildings with silver, especially the church, which recently had been painted white.

A dog began to bark and was immediately answered by a coyote somewhere to the south of the town.

For several minutes Thomas listened to the dialog between the two animals. Though he had no use for coyotes, he couldn't help thinking as he sat hunched forward in his saddle that they were free. Maybe they were really better off than any dog who was forced to depend on his master for his food — or for that matter, his very freedom to roam around the town. Maybe the coyote was telling the dog to run away and join him and the other coyotes, and the dog was answering that he was tethered to a stake out back of some store, or that he was afraid that if he went with the coyotes, he wouldn't be able to fend for himself.

Thomas thought of himself as a coyote — or, more fitting, a wolf. No one ever tethered a wolf, and that was what his father wanted to do to him by forcing him to marry Helen Wicker. Marriage to her would rob him of his freedom and he'd be a tethered dog.

His anger flared and, striking his hand on his thigh, he proclaimed defiantly, 'I'd rather be in hell.'

The sudden outburst made Gray throw up his head and neigh, pawing at the ground nervously.

'Easy there,' Thomas said, patting the horse's neck. 'Easy, Gray.' He continued to speak and pat the animal until it steadied down. 'It's not you I'm angry at, not you at all.'

The dog suddenly began to yelp and then was quiet, but the coyote continued to bark. Thomas shook his head knowingly and he touched his spurs to the animal's flanks. Slowly he worked Gray down the rise to the end of town. A short while later he was riding Gray at a walk along the deserted main street to the Broken Horn Saloon.

He swung out of the saddle and wrapped the reins around the hitching post. Except for the time he had spent eating lunch and dinner, he had been riding since sunup, and that was too many hours to even bother counting. He pulled his shoulders back and rubbed his grimy face with the sleeve streaked with dried blood. Since he didn't have to work for the next couple of days, he could sleep. But if he had to choose between sleeping and making love to Lisa, he had no doubt what his choice would be. He took a few moments to hitch up his pants and set his holster low on his right hip before entering the swinging doors of the Broken Horn Saloon.

There were four men playing poker at a table off to one side near the rear wall. Two trail tramps were drinking at the bar under the hawk-like eyes of Tiny, a slow-moving bull of a man with a soft voice and fists that could crack a man's skull open with one blow.

Thomas made his way to the bar. The clank of his spurs on the hard wood floor caused the men at the table to glance at him for a moment. He knew all of them, and he nodded. The trail tramps waited until he came up to the bar before they gave him the once-over. Thomas didn't bother to look their way since he could see them in the mirror behind the bar.

'Didn't expect to see you here till Saturday night,' Tiny said, planting himself in front of the newcomer.

Thomas nodded but didn't offer any explanation. He put a tight rein on his impulse to ask where Lisa was, and instead asked for whiskey.

Tiny set down a bottle and a shot glass on the bar.

'Thanks,' Thomas said. He poured himself a drink and drank it in one swift gulp. An instant later he could feel it burn its way down his gullet and fire his stomach. He drank another one down as swiftly as the first.

'I hear tell,' Tiny said, looking at Thomas' blood-stained sleeve, 'that the longhorns are meaner than ever.'

'When aren't those critters mean?'

The barkeep chuckled. 'Every spring I hear how mean they are,' he said. 'Seems to me that you cowboys should be used to them by now.'

'When does a man ever get used to playing tag with the devil?'

Tiny's chuckle became a hearty laugh. 'It's a fool who plays with the devil,' he said. 'But each man to his taste. I tend bar, Ross over at the table is a gamblin' man, and you — well, you're not exactly a vaquero but you're a damn good stand-in for one.'

Thomas laughed. 'My pa pays me the same wages he pays the hired hands. Twenty dollars a month, my grub, and a roof over my head.'

'You complainin', are you?'

Thomas fell silent.

'Some day the whole Carey spread will belong to you.' Tiny leaned forward. 'Your pappy is just tryin' you out. I'd do the same if I were in his boots. I bet he still can outride, out-rope and outshoot —' He stopped. 'What I mean,' he hastily explained, 'is that he could still carry his own weight.'

'No one ever said he couldn't,' Thomas answered, aware that the two men at the bar had stopped talking the moment Tiny had mentioned his surname, and that they were looking at his reflection in the mirror.

Had it been another time, he would have turned to them and asked if they knew him or had any questions, or he might have told them he didn't like being stared at. But he didn't want to mix with them. He was too saddle-weary to get into a fight with a couple of trail bums who had nothing better to do than sop up cheap whiskey and look at him. The hell with them! He bolted down another shot.

'That stuff may burn a little goin' down,' Tiny said, referring to the whiskey, 'but don't think that's all it does.'

Thomas realized that the barkeep was giving him some friendly advice. He pushed the bottle back toward the man and with a smile said, 'What do I owe you?'

'Three drinks?'

'Three.'

'A dollar'll do just fine.'

Thomas put a silver dollar down and an additional two bits for a tip.

'Give your father my regards,' Tiny said. 'Don't get much of a chance to see him.'

'He comes into town on Sunday to go to church.'

The barkeep nodded. 'Put up most of the money for its painting,' he said in a respectful voice.

Thomas didn't know that but he shrugged and said, 'He's a believer.'

'Most folks aren't when it comes to their pocket-books,' Tiny said. 'Money is usually what separates those that talk religion and those that practice it.' Then he chuckled and added, 'Money is really what separates most men from what they lay claim to be to what they really are.'

'I guess so,' Thomas commented, and before the barkeep could say anything else about money or religion, he asked about Lisa.

Tiny jerked his head toward the steps that led to the upper story, where the women entertained their customers.

The blood drained from Thomas' face. His lower lip trembled but he was unable to speak.

'Sorry,' Tiny said in a whisper.

Thomas nodded.

'She'll be down in a little while,' the barkeep told him.

TWO

Thomas stood very still. His hands clutched the edge of the bar with such force that his knuckles turned white. He wanted to reach for the whiskey bottle, but was afraid that his hand would tremble. Everything was out of focus, misted over by the combination of his anger and the keen feeling of disappointment.

A minute passed, then another, and one more, while Thomas remained motionless. Other than the booming of his own heart, he heard the ticking of the large clock on the wall above the mirror.

'She wasn't expecting you,' Tiny said in a whisper.

Thomas took a deep breath and, after slowly exhaling, said, 'I know.' He waited a moment before adding, 'Tell her I'll be at her place.'

'Sure!' the barkeep answered with a nod. 'Sure, I'll tell her that.'

'Thanks,' Thomas said and, reaching for the bottle, added, 'I'll have one more before I go.'

Tiny shrugged, but the expression on his jowled face wasn't a happy one.

'One more won't hurt none,' Thomas assured him.

'Maybe yes, maybe no. Sometimes it has to do with the way a man feels when he's drinking.'

Thomas managed a smile as he poured himself a drink. 'I feel fine,' he told the barkeep. 'Just fine.' He bolted the whiskey down in one swallow.

'That's it!' he exclaimed, and stepped back from the bar when he heard one of the trail bums say to the other, 'Ol' Jack is sure gettin' his money's worth from that whore.'

And the other answered, poking his comrade in the ribs with his elbow, 'Maybe I'll give her a try. She looks like she can go at it all night an' still want more come sunup.'

The two men laughed.

'That's the way it is with them Mex women, especially if they got some Injun blood in them. And from the looks of this one I'd bet a month's wages she's got more than a sprinkle.'

Thomas clenched his teeth so hard that slashes of pain cut at the muscles in his jaw. He focused his eyes on the reflection of the two men in the mirror behind the bar. It was the first time since he had seen them that he took the time to look at them.

The man closest to him was short and wiry with a rodent-like face and more than a day's stubble on his chin. He wore a trail-stained planter's hat. The other was taller and lean. His nose was broken and a long white scar cut diagonally down his right cheek. Both men carried holstered guns, and Thomas had no doubt that they knew how to use them.

The taller of the two glanced up and saw that Thomas was looking at him. He pushed his sombrero back on his head and drew back his lips in an ugly smile. With his eyes still on the mirror, he said, 'Ain't that right 'bout Mex women with Injun blood in 'em?' Though he spoke softly, his voice was more of a hiss than a whisper.

Thomas remained silent. His eyes flicked over to Tiny. The barkeep had edged slightly off to the right of where he had been standing. One hand was below the level of the bar.

'Jest like black women,' the shorter one said, 'who have a white daddy or granddaddy!'

'You don't talk much,' the other said, still looking at Thomas in the mirror. 'Boy, didn't your pappy bother teachin' you any manners?'

Thomas' eyes narrowed and he answered, 'I have nothing to say.'

'Is that a fact? From the way you were lookin' at me I thought you did.'

Thomas shook his head. 'You made a mistake,' he told the man.

'Maybe,' the saddle tramp replied, turning to face him. 'But maybe not.'

'He still didn't answer your question, Zeb,' the other one said. 'Seems like he's old enough to give a straight answer.'

'Maybe he didn't hear it,' his partner said.

'I heard!'

'Then answer it.' This time the man's voice was hard and loud.

Thomas was sure that the men at the table had heard him and had probably stopped their playing to see what was happening. He knew they were trying to goad him into a fight, make him go for his gun.

'You have no cause to push me, mister,' he said. 'I don't know you and you don't know me.'

Both men laughed. 'I'm Zeb,' the big man said. 'This is Aron, and Jack, my brother, is upstairs with —'

'I still don't know you,' Thomas said quickly.

Aron snickered. 'Boy, can't you 'ear good? Zeb jest tol' ya our names,' he said. 'Now, don't be mule-headed, answer his question.'

Thomas said nothing.

'Maybe you ain't man enough to answer it?' Zeb said. 'Or maybe you got a special reason —' The sound of a door opening and closing stopped him. He glanced at Aron. 'Jack,' he said.

'More'n likely,' Aron replied.

Spurs clanked against the wooden floor. The steps creaked as the man came down. Thomas got a good look at him as he passed and went up to the bar. Aron moved away from Zeb to make room for him.

Jack was a chunky man, with a weather-beaten, pockmarked face straddled by a wide-brimmed hat from Kansas way. His gun was low on his right hip.

'Where's the woman?' Zeb asked.

'She'll be down directly,' Jack answered.

'I think I'll try her.'

Jack shrugged and looked at Thomas and then at his brother.

'I asked him a question,' Zeb quickly explained, 'and he doesn't have manners enough to answer it.'

Jack's face hardened. 'I told the two of you not to go gettin' into a fight.'

'A man ain't a man less'n he can talk to other men like a man,' Zeb said.

'Leave him be,' Jack said. Then, looking at Thomas, he told him that his brother didn't mean any harm, that he was just quick to take offense and hot-tempered.

Thomas nodded.

'Jest to show you there's no hard feelin',' Jack said, 'come have a drink with us.'

Thomas hesitated.

'C'mon,' Jack said, gesturing him to where he and the others stood. 'Drinkin' together is a right good way to —'

'There's the woman!' Zeb exclaimed. 'Don't she look a sight?'

Thomas turned toward the steps. Even though Lisa was some distance from him, he could see there were blue welts on her arms and her face was red and puffy from crying.

Lisa saw him. 'Thomas!' she exclaimed. 'Why —' And she started toward him.

'Not him!' Zeb shouted. 'I got next call on you.'

Lisa stopped and looked questioningly at Thomas.

'I got next call on her,' Zeb insisted. 'But will you look at the way she looks at him?'

'Lisa,' Thomas said softly, 'stay where you are.'

'So that's how it is!' Jack exclaimed.

'I tried to tell you,' Zeb said, 'but you wouldn't listen. She's his woman. An' I ask't 'im if Mex women with Injun blood ain't the best whores, even better than a black woman with white blood.'

'She your'n?' Jack asked, looking at Thomas.

'Lisa,' Thomas said, ignoring the question, 'go back upstairs.'

'Now jest a minute, boy!' Jack exclaimed. 'You got no cause to take on so about a whore. Zeb won't take long and then you can have 'er, that's if Aron don't want 'er. Now you tell 'er to come here and let Zeb get a good look at what he's buyin'. Fair is fair. No man wants a pig in a poke, now ain't that right?'

'She's going back upstairs,' Thomas said slowly and very quietly. Each word possessed a white heat of its own and burned through the space between him and the three men.

'You're mighty sure of yourself,' Jack said.

'Sure enough!'

'All right,' Jack told Zeb, 'let her go.' And he started to turn back to the bar.

It was too easy! A man like Jack was not likely to back down without a fight. Thomas watched him. His body was tense and his mind alert. Then he saw it: Zeb had moved slightly to the left of his brother to give him just enough room to wheel around and make his play.

Thomas kept his attention on the three men. He was sure Tiny had one hand on a gun, but he didn't want the barkeep mixing in his fight.

'Seems to me,' Jack started to say, 'that your pappy should 'ave taught you some respect.' The moment he finished speaking his hand went to his gun. It cleared the holster just as he swung around. The room quivered from the explosion of his first shot. It smashed into the far wall.

Thomas reacted the instant he saw Jack's hand move. His gun was out. He dropped to the floor and fired. A second explosion shook the room. A tongue of flame leaped from the muzzle of the Navy Colt. Smoke hung close to the floor.

The .36 slug slammed into Jack's chest, knocking him back against the bar. He looked surprised. The gun fell from his hand and he slid to the floor.

Thomas was on his feet before either Zeb or Aron could move. A thin wisp of gray smoke curled from the muzzle of his Navy Colt. The room was filled with the sharp smell of burned powder.

Zeb looked down at his brother and then at Thomas. 'You killed 'im!' he shouted. 'Never even gave 'im a chance.'

'It was a fair fight,' Tiny said, 'Jack drew first.'

'I won't forget this,' Zeb said. 'I'll make you wish —'

'Move!' Thomas ordered. 'Get out of here and take him with you.'

'By the living God,' Zeb said, 'I swear I'll make you pay for this.' Then he and Aron lifted Jack's body and carried it out of the Broken Horn.

As soon as they were gone the men at the table crowded around Thomas. Slapping him on the back, they praised his coolness, his shooting, but most of all his lightning-like draw. He shook them off and made his way to the steps where Lisa was standing.

She had witnessed the shooting, and when he came to her she threw herself into his arms and cried, '*Madre de Dios*, I thought he kilt you.'

'He didn't,' Thomas said flatly. 'Now get your things, I'll take you home.'

'*Sí,*' she answered. '*Sí!*' And she hurried up the steps.

Thomas went back to the bar. All of the men were drinking and though they offered to buy, Thomas refused. He motioned Tiny aside and said, 'I didn't want to —'

'Makes little difference,' the barkeep told him. 'You did, and now those two will be lookin' for you.'

'I guess so.'

'Don't fret. Sooner or later he would have tangled with someone who was a better gun.'

Thomas nodded and then said, 'I'm not fretting about it. Like you said, he drew first. But I don't feel anything. Do you know what I mean?'

Tiny shook his head. 'No,' he said, 'whenever I had to kill I always felt sick inside afterwards.'

'Even when —?'

'Always,' Tiny answered. Then he said, 'Lisa is waiting for you by the steps.'

'Thanks,' Thomas said, turned and walked rapidly toward Lisa.

Even as Thomas started to unhitch Gray, Mr Wyler, the sheriff, came running down the street, buckling his gun belt. Wyler had come to Paso Diablo about five years before. He was kind of a drifter, doing short stints of work as far west as the Pecos River and north to the Red. Around that time he was beginning to feel too old for herding cows and was looking for a place to settle down. The sheriff's job was open when he came and he applied for it, never really thinking he would get it. He was a good man with a horse, a good roper, but never much to shout about when it came to using a gun.

'Heard the shots,' Wyler said, breathing hard. 'What's it all about?'

'Tiny will tell you,' Thomas answered.

Wyler was a short chunky man and he tilted his head back to squint up at Thomas. 'I think you better come with me,' he said.

'No reason to,' he told Wyler. 'The man drew on me —'

'An' you shot 'im?'

'That's the size of it.'

'*Sí*,' Lisa said. *'El hombre malo!'*

Wyler ignored Lisa and kept his eyes on Thomas. 'You comin' with me?' he asked.

'I'll be around town for the next few days.'

The sheriff glanced at Lisa and then back at Thomas. 'At her place?'

'Yes.'

'Know who it was?' Wyler asked.

'Went by the name of Jack. There were two others with him. One was called Zeb and the other Aron. None of them come from around here.'

'I warned you the last time you got into a gunfight that I wasn't goin' to let it pass.'

Thomas nodded. 'I wasn't looking for a fight. Ask Tiny,' he told the sheriff. 'I didn't want trouble.'

'For a man who don't want trouble you sure find it.'

'I don't look for it,' Thomas answered stubbornly.

'Where are the other two?'

Thomas shrugged. 'They took off after the shooting.'

'And the dead man?'

'Took him with them.'

Wyler shook his head. 'Your pa ain't goin' to like this one bit,' he said. 'Not one bit.' Then he turned and stomped up the two steps and into the Broken Horn.

'You think he will make trouble?' Lisa asked as Thomas picked her up and set her side-saddle on Gray.

'No,' he answered, swinging on to his horse. 'Tiny will tell him what happened, and so will the other men.'

Lisa heaved a deep sigh and went limp against him. 'I was so scared,' she whispered. 'When you fell to the floor —'

'Makes no sense to chew it over,' he told her, and, circling her waist with his right hand, he guided Gray down the main street toward the creek at the edge of the town.

'Why did you come tonight?' she asked.

Thomas shrugged but said nothing. When he had looked down on Paso Diablo from the knoll, outside of town, he had thought of telling her about his argument with his father. But somehow he felt that to explain anything would be a sign of weakness, even more than his coming to see her.

She did not repeat the question and did not speak again until they came within sight of the shanty. 'Simon will be asleep,' she said.

'I'll be quiet,' Thomas told her. Then he asked, 'Does he mind when I come?'

Lisa looked up at him. 'He feels toward you like a brother,' she answered. 'He is almost a man, and knows that a man needs a woman.'

'I feel toward him like a brother too,' he said, halting Gray in front of the door.

She reached up and kissed him on the cheek. 'He knows that,' she whispered, and then she slid down from the saddle. A moment later she went into the shanty.

Thomas dismounted, led Gray into the shed and unsaddled him. When he had provided sufficient feed and water for the animal, he swung his saddle on to his shoulder and entered the shanty. Lisa had already lit a Betty lamp and was putting another log on the fire.

Thomas lowered his saddle to the floor at the side of the door and then stood very still for a few moments. The shanty was part wood, part sod. Simon slept off to the right of the big room that served as kitchen and dining room. The fireplace was crude. The ceiling was low and blackened with smoke. The table and chairs were second-hand. He himself had bought them at the general store. The room he shared with Lisa was curtained off from the rest of the place by an old Indian blanket. It was only large enough to hold a big brass bed and a small chest of drawers.

'Next time I come,' he said, crossing the floor to where Lisa was standing, 'I'll bring you a fancy lamp.'

'Who's there?' Simon called from the darkened corner where he slept.

'Go back to sleep!' Lisa told her brother.

'It's me, Thomas.'

The boy raised himself up. 'Was there shooting in town?' he asked. 'I was sure I heard two shots.'

'*Vamos a dormir,*' Lisa told him.

'*No! Digame!*'

'There's nothing to tell,' Thomas said. 'At least not anything that can't wait until morning.'

'*Mañana!*' Lisa exclaimed impatiently and, picking up the crude lamp, motioned Thomas to follow her.

Simon grumbled, but slipped down on to his pallet again.

Thomas followed Lisa into her portion of the shanty. She set the lamp down on the chest of drawers and said, 'I want to wash first.'

He nodded and sat down on the bed. A moment later she was gone. He knew that she would go down to the creek, strip off her clothes, and dive into the icy water. When she'd come back to him, her body would be cleansed of —

Thomas stopped and heaved a deep sigh. For him to think of her befouled by the embraces of other men served no purpose, and would probably put him in an ugly mood by the time she returned. He bent down and slipped off his boots. Then he stood up, took off his gun belt and put it on the chest with the gun half-drawn from the holster. He removed his buckskin jacket and shotgun chaps, untied his wipe, and finally took off his shirt. He put all four on a wall peg.

For a moment he considered going down to the creek to join Lisa, but the sure knowledge that the water would be icy cold stopped him. He dropped down on to the bed and stretched out on the lumpy mattress. For a while he watched the yellow lamplight flicker on the low ceiling. Then he moved his eyes to the corner of the room where the Indian blanket was. He had been meaning to put up a door but somehow never got around to it.

That was an excuse and he knew it. Thomas slipped his hands behind his head. Whenever he came to see Lisa, it was for one reason only. He might have thought about putting up a door, fixing the roof, or doing several other things to make the place more comfortable; but the moment he saw her, all his good intentions, his high resolve, was consumed like so much dry kindling by the fire in his groin. That was the way it was when it came to her, and there was nothing he could do, or wanted to do, to change it.

Sometimes it almost seemed to him that she had put one of those crazy Indian spells on him for having taken her when she was still young. If he hadn't, some Mex or ranch-hand would have; maybe even some Indian buck would have wrassled her down and raped her. At least he didn't do that. He made love to her just the way he had to any of the women he ever had. And she didn't say no, or fight too hard to free herself. After all, not only was he a gringo but he was the son of the wealthiest gringo…

Thomas rolled his head toward the wall. His thoughts were becoming ornery. The truth of the matter was that he had made her his whore, and when her folks died she had taken the job at the Broken Horn. If anyone had reason to hate him, she did. But she loved him, maybe even more than he loved her.

The lamplight suddenly began to flicker. For a moment Thomas thought it was going to go out, but then he realized the cause and, turning away from the wall, looked toward the Indian blanket. Lisa had pushed it aside to enter her room.

'How was your bath?' he asked, as he watched her hang her clothes on the wall pegs next to his. She was wearing a shapeless, long-sleeved, high-necked muslin nightgown that reached down to the floor. Her black hair spilled halfway down her back, and in the dim light her face was the color of polished brass.

'Cold,' she replied without looking at him.

'I thought so!'

She faced him and said, 'I'm clean now.'

Thomas pushed himself up and reached out toward her. *Te quiero,*' he whispered. 'I want you.'

She hung back. 'Why did you come tonight?' she asked.

He dropped his hands. 'Why the question? Isn't it enough to know that I want you?'

'*Sí,*' she answered after a moment's hesitation, and she leaned toward the Betty lamp to blow it out.

'No,' Thomas said. 'Don't.'

She looked questioningly at him.

'I want to see you.'

Lisa smiled. 'You have already seen everything.' But even as she spoke, her hands were busy opening the row of four buttons down the front of the nightgown.

Thomas watched her, and when the garment drifted to the floor, leaving her naked before him, he devoured her body with his eyes. 'Now you can douse the light,' he said. An instant later the room was plunged into darkness, and then he felt the softness of her body against him. He sighed deeply and kissed her lips.

'*Te quiero,*' she cried, as their bodies came together. '*Te quiero muchísimo!*'

Though he had experienced the delirium of pleasure with her before, it had never been as wild as this. Never had she given herself to him with such intense abandon. And even as he found fulfillment in her body he sensed that the intensity of her passion was in some strange way connected to the gunfight he had had at the Broken Horn. Was she expressing her gratitude or did it have something to do with the fact that he had killed a man? No matter what the cause, all that mattered to Thomas was the shuddering pleasure of the moment.

By the time Thomas left Lisa's bed and went down to the creek to wash, the sun was already high in the morning sky. The day was bright and unseasonably warm. Thomas stripped down and swam in the creek, enjoying the sting of the icy water.

When he returned to the shanty, Lisa was up and fixing breakfast. She looked none the worse for the previous night's violent lovemaking. If anything, she seemed oddly subdued, almost content.

'Coffee will be ready soon,' she told him as he passed through the main room and went into her room for the rest of his gear. It took him a few minutes to don his chaps and put on his gun belt. When he returned, he sat down at the table and asked where Simon was, since he had not seen him earlier and he was not around now.

'He is working at the blacksmith's,' she said.

'Bueno!' he answered with a smile.

'He does not like it,' Lisa told him with a shrug.

'Why not?' Thomas asked, intensely aware of the way her full breasts rolled under the muslin gown when she shrugged.

'He wants to be a vaquero,' she said, 'like you.'

Thomas laughed.

'It is not funny,' she said. Then with another shrug she added. 'He will be what he will be. I cannot stop him.'

'There's nothing wrong with being a ranch hand,' he said defensively.

'Not for a man,' she answered, looking straight at him. 'But it is no good for a woman. The vaquero *es un animal. Malo, muy malo.'*

Thomas finally understood and was embarrassed. 'Maybe if I talked to him,' he offered, 'he'll change his mind.'

She nodded and took the coffee pot off the grate in the fireplace. After she had filled two mugs, she sat down facing Thomas. The coffee was very hot and steam rose from its surface. 'You think,' she said looking at him, 'the other two will come back?'

He knew she meant Zeb and Aron. He shook his head. 'Not likely,' he assured her.

'The brot'er of the man you shot said 'e'd come back.'

'Just talk,' Thomas replied, and then remembered there were only four shots left in his gun. He drew it and slipped the cylinder out of the frame. 'I better load the other chamber,' he said, and went to his saddlebags to get the things he needed. He set them out on the table and quickly began to roll a piece of heavy paper around a wooden dowel. When that was done he closed one end of it with bootmaker's thread, dropped a lead ball into it and tied it off with a loop of thread. Then he added the powder, twisted the open end into a pig's tail and folded it back against the side of the part that held the powder. When he was finished he held it up and examined it. Satisfied, he slipped it into the empty chamber and replaced the cylinder into the frame of the gun.

Lisa watched him without speaking, but as soon as he set the gun back in the holster she said, 'Tell me why you came last night.'

He looked at her for a moment, then picked up the equipment he had used to make another bullet and returned it to his saddlebag. When he came back to the table he said, 'I had some words with my pa.' He lifted his mug and began to drink. The coffee was still hot and brewed strong the way he liked it.

'*No comprendo,*' she said.

'An argument,' he replied. He was annoyed with her for asking the same question so many times. 'Damn it!' he exclaimed. 'Are you going to start pushing at me too?'

'Your pa knows about me?'

Thomas cocked his head to one side. 'Sure he knows,' he said. 'Everyone around here knows.'

She nodded, and left the table to get the ham and eggs from the blackened iron frying pan. She set the pan on the table and told him to help himself.

After he had taken what he wanted he asked her if she wanted him to give her some.

'I'm not hungry,' she said.

He didn't answer and began to eat. He could sense they were headed toward a fracas, and it made him lose his appetite. He hadn't even finished half the food on his plate when he pushed it away from him.

'Your pa doesn't want you to see me anymore?' she said.

'Are you telling me or asking me?'

She shrugged and said, 'I know.'

Thomas bolted to his feet so quickly that he almost overturned the table. 'What do you know?' he asked harshly. 'What the hell do you know?' And he began pacing back and forth.

'Why are you angry at me?'

He stopped and glared at her. 'I don't like questions,' he told her, 'from you, my pa, or anyone else.' He started to pace again. A few moments later he stopped. 'Just because I sleep with you don't think you have any call on me.'

'*Te quiero*,' she said in a choked whisper.

'*Te quiero*,' he mimicked and added, 'Sure, you want —'

'I love you, Thomas,' she whimpered.

'Like you do all the other men who give you money,' he challenged.

Tears streamed down her cheeks.

'Your bawling won't change matters,' he said. 'Maybe my pa is right. Maybe I should marry the Wicker girl and get the hell away from you.'

Lisa gasped.

'That's what he wants me to do,' Thomas shouted at her. And then taking a deep breath, he said, 'Now you know why I came to see you last night.' He pulled the chair away from the table and flung himself into it.

'And what did you tell 'im?' she asked, after a long silence.

'Nothing,' he said. 'He told me that I have three days to make up my mind. If I don't decide to marry the Wicker girl he doesn't want me to go back to the ranch.'

'Oh, Thomas,' she cried, and hurried around the table to where he sat. 'He's your pa,' she said, putting her arms around his neck. 'He doesn't mean it.'

He wrenched himself free of her embrace and said, 'Make no mistake, my pa is a man of his word. He meant everything he said. He has no use for your kind of woman, and he hasn't got much use for me. The only things that really matter to him are his precious name, the cattle and land he owns, and his God.'

Lisa moved away from him. In all the years that he had been coming to her she had never heard him speak about his father, and now that he was, she was frightened by the naked anger that she saw.

Thomas stood up and faced her. 'If my pa had his way you and all the other women at the Broken Horn would be stoned to death. He's a man of faith, a true believer in the torments of fire and brimstone that await the sinful —' He stopped and began to laugh. 'I can just see his face when he finds out that I was in another gunfight.'

'And you will see it,' she said.

Her words quenched his anger. He looked at her and with a nod said, 'Yes, I will see it!'

'You will marry the Wicker girl?'

He nodded and said, 'But that doesn't mean I can't see you.'

The back of her hand flew to her mouth and she ran to her room behind the Indian curtain.

For a few moments everything was quiet, then Thomas heard the sound of Lisa's sobbing. He started to go to her and then stopped, turned and went to the door. He looked back at the Indian blanket. This was not the way he had wanted things to happen. Maybe he had known what would happen the moment Tiny had told him that Lisa was upstairs with a man?

He shook his head. Reaching down for his saddle, he swung it up on his shoulder. Then he opened the door and walked out into the hot sun.

THREE

Thomas rode up the main street of Paso Diablo to the sheriff's office. News of the gunfight and its outcome had spread all over the small town. Thomas sensed that the men in front of Broken Horn and the few women on the street were looking at him with a strange mixture of fascination and horror. One woman pulled her small son behind the protective covering of the door to the general store, even though the child struggled to be free.

When he reached his destination he dismounted and looped the reins around the hitching post. Then he walked up to the door of the sheriff's office and knocked.

'Come in,' Wyler called. 'It's open.'

Thomas entered the office. The sheriff sat behind the desk. He looked up.

'I'm going back to the ranch,' Thomas said, not wanting to waste words. Then he added, 'Unless you tell me I have to stay in town.'

Wyler stood up. 'No reason for you to stay here,' he said.

Thomas nodded, then turned and started back to the door.

'Wait a minute,' Wyler said.

Thomas stopped and faced him.

'The man you killed and the other two with him —'

'What about them?'

'They work for Johnson,' Wyler told him. 'If I were you I'd keep away from them.'

'I won't go looking for them,' Thomas said. 'But I won't turn tail and run if they come looking for me.'

'I don't want any more killin',' Wyler said.

'There'll be none,' Thomas answered, 'unless they start.'

'Your pa and some other ranchers around these parts don't like Johnson —'

Thomas smiled. 'I can't say that I blame them,' he said. 'On more than one roundup I've seen their hands cut out critters to make up their herd that rightfully belonged to my pa or some of the other ranches around here. They'd be out on the range putting the Johnson brand on everything they could find, sometimes as much as a week before the real roundup started.'

Wyler nodded. 'I don't speak highly of Johnson's actions but there ain't no law that says a rancher has to work with other ranchers on a roundup. The herd, except those critters with brands on them, can be worked by anyone.'

'Then maybe there should be a law.'

'Until there is,' Wyler said, 'Johnson is free to do what he wants.'

Thomas didn't answer. The sheriff was entitled to his opinion and he would respect it. But if any of the Johnson hands strayed into the part of the range that he and others like him were working there would be trouble, law or no law. So far Johnson had been smart enough to keep his men as far away as possible from the other ranchers.

'Just don't go lookin' for a fight,' Wyler said.

'I won't.'

Wyler nodded and said, 'Send my regards to your pa.'

'Thanks,' Thomas said. He turned and quickly left the office. A few moments later he was back in the saddle and on his way to the Broken Horn Saloon, diagonally across the street. Once more he dismounted and tied the reins to the hitching post. He paused long enough to pat the flank of the animal. Gray turned his head and nuzzled him. 'We'll be on our way home soon,' he whispered, and walked up the steps.

Tiny was already on duty behind the bar. An early drinker sat off to one side with a bottle and a glass in front of him. He didn't even look up as Thomas crossed the room to the bar.

'Saw you ride in,' Tiny said, as Thomas came up to the bar.

'I went to see the sheriff.'

The barkeep nodded and said, 'Me and some of the other boys told him how it happened.'

'Thanks.'

'The three of them rode for Johnson.'

'Two,' Thomas said, correcting him. 'The other one is either in heaven or hell.'

'My guess,' Tiny commented, 'is that he'll have to serve his time in hell before he gets to the other place.'

'I'm going back to the ranch,' Thomas told him.

The barkeep smiled. 'Will you be in again come Saturday night?' he asked.

Thomas shook his head. 'Probably not,' he said.

'Lisa —'

'I won't be in,' Thomas said harshly, and then his voice softened. 'I didn't mean to harden up on you,' he explained, 'but things just aren't working out the way I thought they would.'

'Sometimes,' Tiny commented philosophically, 'it goes that way. A man's got to learn to live with the good and the bad.'

'I guess so,' Thomas replied. Desperately he wanted to tell Tiny what had happened between him and Lisa, but knew that if he did the both of them would be too embarrassed to ever look at the other again or remain friends. 'See you,' he said nonchalantly, and walked out of the Broken Horn.

Thomas rode slowly back to the ranch house. By the time he arrived the sun was well past the midway point in the sky, and to shield his eyes from its brightness he wore his sombrero low over his forehead. Now and then in the distance he saw a sudden cloud of dust erupt from the dun-colored plain and he knew that one or more ranch hands were busy moving a stray out of a coulee or bringing one out of the brush. Though it was second nature with him — as it was with every ranch hand — to notice everything in sight, Thomas was really occupied with the thoughts running through his own brain like a stampeding herd.

Nothing seemed to make much sense. Had he stayed in Paso Diablo with Lisa he would have been wrong. And sooner or later he knew he would have become involved in another gunfight because of her. Maybe he would even have taken to hard drinking. Many a man wound up with his guts rotted out from too much bad whiskey. He did not want that to happen to him, but marrying the Wicker girl didn't seem to offer anything more appealing. Sure, he'd have a place of his own and stock of his own. That would give him something for marrying a woman for whom he had no feelings. No matter how he looked at his future, it seemed to be filled with black storm clouds and flashing lightning.

As soon as Gray crested the ridge and sensed he was close to home he broke into a fast trot. Thomas gave the animal his head, and a short time later he rode into the front yard. Gray headed straight for the stable, and as soon as he reached it he stopped. Thomas dismounted, led him inside, and unsaddled him. As soon as that was done, he took time to water and grain him. Only when Gray was properly tended, even to the extent of curry-combing the animal, did he place him in his stall and leave the stable.

Thomas was halfway to the house when he saw his father ride into the yard. The old man passed him without saying a word and Thomas continued to walk to the house.

'Is that you, Señor William?' Maria called from the kitchen.

Thomas didn't answer. He was sure that she was calling his father.

'*Thomas no ha regresado,*' she said, poking her head out into the dining room. When she saw him she gave a small cry of surprise and, like a turtle, pulled her head back into the kitchen.

He went to his room, stripped down to the waist, and washed the dust from his face. Then he put his shirt back on, took his Makin's out of the breast pocket and rolled a cigarette. To light it, he went back into the main room and, with a pair of tongs, lifted a glowing ember from the fireplace. The end of the paper flared and the loosely packed tobacco started to burn. He took two deep drags on it to make sure that it was lit and then dropped the ember back into the fireplace and replaced the tongs in the rack.

The smell of Maria's cooking stirred his appetite, and he suddenly remembered he had had damn little to eat. He went to the kitchen door and asked, 'What's for dinner?'

Maria was middle-aged with a build like a pouter pigeon. She was married to Victor Gonzalez, one of the oldest hands on the ranch. Thomas had known her all his life. She had often tended him when he was sick, and his feelings for her were warm.

'For you, not'in',' she said, with a toss of her head.

'Not even if I tell you I haven't eaten anything all day?' he asked, suppressing a smile.

She glared at him. 'No one told you to go ridin' off to Paso Diablo,' she scolded. '*No eso niño chiquito.*'

He shook his head. 'That's right, and I'm hungry as a man, maybe two men. Now tell me what smells so good?'

'Pollo.'

'And?'

'Chuleta de puerco.'

Thomas took the cigarette out of his mouth and licked his lips. 'I smell something else,' he said. 'What is it?'

'Fresh bread and pie.'

He smiled broadly.

'Vamos!' she exclaimed, and she gestured for him to leave.

'Sí,' Thomas said. 'But you know I couldn't stay away from your cooking.' Chuckling to himself, he returned to the main room. Maria was one person who always made him feel good.

He went to the window and looked across the front yard to the stable. His father was taking a particularly long time to put up his horse. Maybe the old man was having trouble figuring out what he should say to him. But Thomas doubted it. Then the stable door opened and his father came out.

Thomas watched him. Though he kept his back straight, William walked with the slow, rolling gait of an old man. When his father came close to the house Thomas moved away from the window and stood close to the fireplace.

The door opened and William entered the room. He threw a quick glance at his son and said, 'Seems like you did more than pay a visit to that whore in Paso Diablo.'

'I was going to tell you about it,' Thomas explained.

'News, especially that kind, moves fast. How many of Johnson's hands did you kill?'

'One.'

William snorted. 'I was told three,' he said. 'By tomorrow it will be six.'

'I wasn't looking for trouble,' Thomas answered, dragging hard on his cigarette.

'Never do,' the old man flashed back. 'With your kind it just seems to happen.'

Thomas ripped the cigarette from his lips and tossed it into the hearth. He had come home, but not to be scolded like a child or to be preached to. 'The man drew on me —'

William held up his hand. 'What's done is done,' he said. 'I'm not interested in how it happened or why.' His eyes narrowed down to the size of a gimlet's. 'Are you staying?' he asked, aware that there was more than just a nervous quiver in the sound of his voice.

Thomas nodded.

'That's not enough!' his father exclaimed. 'I want a firm "yes" from you. Forget that you're my son and give me your word as a man.'

'Yes, damn it. Yes!'

'One would have been sufficient,' the old man said, and then he went to the shelf at the far end of the room where the family Bible was kept. He picked it up and walked back to where his son stood. 'You swear on the Good Book,' he said, holding it in front of Thomas.

'I gave you my word.'

'Swear!'

Thomas shook his head. 'No!'

'Swear!' William repeatedly angrily. That he should have raised a son without the fear of God in him was surely a burden too heavy for his shoulders to bear.

'I gave you my word,' Thomas answered stubbornly. He glared at his father. The man wanted too much. He always wanted too much from him. Even when he was a boy his father had made him do a man's work. 'That book,' Thomas said in a low but determined voice, 'is yours. It is not mine. You put your faith in it. I can't.'

William flushed. 'Those are terrible words,' he answered, but he sensed that to push his son any further would end any hope he still had for the boy's future. He lowered the Bible slowly. 'I'll take your word,' he said with a deep sigh, and returned the Bible to its place on the shelf.

Thomas breathed easier.

'I want to wash,' his father said as he returned from the other side of the room. 'Then we'll have dinner.'

'That's fine with me,' Thomas answered. 'I haven't had much to eat all day.'

The old man cocked his head to one side and was about to comment that his son never did show much common sense, but thought better of it and went to his room without saying anything.

After dinner, William filled his corncob pipe and smoked it for a while without speaking. He knew what he wanted to say to Thomas but wasn't at all sure about how to put the words together. Then finally he said, 'Tomorrow I'll write to Clem and tell him to try and get home in time for your wedding.'

Thomas nodded.

'Is the middle of June all right with you?'

'Yes.'

'I married your mother in June,' the old man said. 'Most women like to get married then.'

'I never gave it much thought.'

'Sunday,' William said, 'I want you to come to church with me —'

'Pa, you know how I feel about church.'

'Helen will be there,' William told him. 'And after church we'll ride back to the Wicker place for Sunday dinner. I think it would be a good idea for you and Helen to spend some time together. As it is, with the roundup and the drive to Austin, you won't have much of a chance to see her.'

Thomas carefully rolled a cigarette and lit it from one of the candles on the table. 'I guess that makes sense,' he said.

'You know,' William said in a soft, confidential voice, 'when a man and a woman live together for a spell, things happen between them that neither of them would have figured could … I mean, people get used to one another, come to depend on each other and grow to be friends. And when the first child comes, they really have something in common.'

Thomas nodded and said, 'Being friends isn't the same as being in love.'

The old man waved the comment aside. 'Sometimes being friends is more important,' William told his son. 'But even love can come if you both try.'

Thomas remained silent. For a few moments he remembered how he had felt when Lisa had stood naked before him. He had wanted her so much that he had actually felt it in his gut. But that feeling could not have been love … it could not have been. And yet …

A stab of longing drove through his groin and he shut his eyes.

'Are you feeling all right?' his father asked.

'Just tired,' he answered, opening his eyes and looking at the old man. 'I think I'll go outside for some fresh air and then turn in.'

'I don't reckon you got much sleep in Paso Diablo,' William commented.

'No, Father, I was busy with other things,' Thomas replied as he stood up.

'There's just one more thing,' the old man said looking up at his son, who had moved to the side of the table.

'And what's that?'

'You know Sam Wicker is the only man in these parts who has slaves?'

'I know that,' Thomas answered. 'I never did understand that.'

William studied his son for several moments before he said, 'Can't expect every man to have the same ways.'

'Then why are you trying so hard to sell him to me?'

'You sure don't give a man much leeway,' the old man said.

'No more or less than you give me.'

'All right then,' his father said, 'I'll put it to you straight. Sam aims to keep his slaves.'

Thomas shrugged. 'I wasn't thinking of taking them away from him,' he replied.

William got to his feet. 'I don't hold with keeping slaves,' he said. 'My granddaddy was a bondsman and worked to buy his freedom. But I don't hold with the abolitionists from the North who are trying to tell us what to do.'

'You're always telling me what to do,' Thomas shot at him, 'even to making me marry —'

'You're my son and what I tell you is for your own good.'

'Maybe you don't know what my good is?'

'Hear me out!' William exclaimed, exasperated by the way his son had twisted the conversation away from the point he was trying to make. 'I don't want you to go running off at the mouth about how you feel toward slavery. Sam can become damn mean when he thinks someone is threatening his property.'

'Strikes me,' Thomas chuckled, 'that a man who owns slaves has picked himself a mighty poor way to show he's a man.'

'And what about a man who has to kill to show that he's a man?' William challenged.

His father's words were razor sharp and they cut him deeply. But rather than start another wrangle between them, Thomas backed down. 'I'll keep clear of the subject,' he said.

'See that you do.'

'Are there any other dos and don'ts?' Thomas asked. 'I'd rather know them all now.'

William shook his head. 'Just be grateful that you have the chance to marry a decent woman and make something of yourself,' he said.

'I'm God-awful grateful!' he said with a harsh, bitter laugh. Then he crossed the room to the door, opened it, and walked out into the front yard.

As soon as William heard the door close he left the table and crossed the room to where the Bible lay. He took it from the shelf and went back to the table. Opening the book to Luke, chapter fifteen, verse eleven, he began to slowly read the parable of the Prodigal Son. When he finished William closed the book and, bowing his head, silently thanked God for having returned his son.

Thomas walked to the fence and, resting his arms on it, leaned forward. His eyes scanned the stretch in front of the low bluish-colored mountains. It was almost perfectly flat except for the rise off to the far right. On the other side of it was Paso Diablo.

He thought about Lisa and realized that he had been cruel to her, but there was little he could do about it. He had given his father his word and he would try to keep it. Besides, he was certain she would not be without a man for long. That another man would know her as he had known her made him even more miserable than he had been.

To stop himself thinking about Lisa he left the fence and walked into the stable. Gray saw him and gave a friendly snort. Thomas patted the animal's head and said, 'Well, ol' boy, come June and I'll be a married man!'

The horse lifted its head.

'That's the way it's going to be … I guess there's no sense either of us kicking up our heels, is there?'

Gray lowered his head and made soft, throaty sounds.

Thomas rubbed the animal's muzzle and said, 'If I was half the man I think I am I'd leave. But this place is as much mine as it is his. Too much of my sweat is here to give it up.'

By the time Thomas left the stable a bright silver-colored moon hung low in the night sky. For an instant Thomas looked at it and then walked slowly back to the house. The main room was empty and the table had been cleared.

Thomas went to his room and removed his gun belt and chaps. He rolled another cigarette and smoked it. Then he stripped down to his underwear and stretched out on the bed.

For a while Thomas lay with his hands tucked under his head. He felt as if there were two people inside of him. One realized his father was doing the right thing, and the other kept hoping something would happen that wouldn't tie him to a woman for whom he had no feelings.

After a while his eyelids became heavy. He was tired of listening to the two voices inside of his brain argue. His eyes closed, and like a stone falling down a well Thomas dropped into a deep and untroubled sleep.

FOUR

The next afternoon the sky turned the color of lead and a cold wind blew out of the north. Thomas and one of the other hands, a man named Rusty, were moving a half-dozen strays out of an arroyo. Once they worked the critters to the funnel-like mouth of the gully, one of the bunch — a twist-horn ladinos — broke from the others and started to jackrabbit across the plain.

'I'll get him,' Thomas yelled to Rusty, and swung Gray around.

The twist-horn was fast and smart. He zigzagged across the open plain, trying to reach an area heavy with brush, where he would be relatively safe. But the cow pony was smarter and quicker. Once he sensed what the twist-horn was trying to do, he cut off to the left. The ladinos saw his escape route to the brush blocked, and immediately veered away and went for the series of deep gullies on the far right.

Thomas let his mount make all the moves. The contest now was between the horse and the twist-horn. His time would come once the twist-horn was either cut off from the gullies or was just too tired to continue the contest. In the meantime, the cow pony was doing what he had been trained to do, and he did it with superb skill.

Once more the horse swung wide of the twist-horn and cut him off from the gullies. Suddenly the ladinos stopped, shook his head, and bawled. The cow pony began to move slowly toward him. Thomas patted the animal's sweaty neck, bent slightly forward and said, 'We've got him now, boy. Just take it easy.'

The twist-horn shook his head again, and his long, twisted horns looked like ugly spears. Thomas watched him intently. Should the critter suddenly decide to charge, he had to be ready to sideslip the animal. From the looks of him Thomas guessed that maybe he was six years old. That would mean that he had eluded twelve roundups.

When he was a few yards from the twist-horn the critter bawled at them, swung around and started to trot. Thomas moved right behind him, and a short time later he had worked the critter back into the bunch that had been in the arroyo.

'Gave you a run,' Rusty laughed when Thomas came up to him.

'Not any more than I expected,' he answered. Then he added, 'I guess we should work this bunch to the main herd.'

'I'll ride drag,' Rusty said.

Thomas nodded and they separated. As soon as they got the bunch started, the twist-horn took up the lead position and the other critters followed along. Neither Thomas nor Rusty had to do much to keep any of the stock from straying, and in less than an hour they hooked up with the main herd.

A short time after Thomas and Rusty had moved their bunch in with the main herd, it started to rain. Both men paused to untie their ponchos from the backs of their saddles and slip them on. At first the rain was nothing more than a thin drizzle, but then it came down in big wind-blown drops, forcing both men to bend low in their saddles.

'Don't think we'll be able to find anything in this rain,' Rusty said.

Thomas agreed and told the ranch hand to ride back to the bunkhouse.

'Where you goin'?' Rusty asked.

'To my father,' Thomas shouted above the sound of the wind and the rain. 'I think he's over on the west range.'

'All right!' Rusty called, and swung his mount around. A moment later he was lost in the downpour.

Though the poncho kept him dry, Thomas was blinded by the pelting rain, and decided to give up the idea of riding to the west range and return home instead. By the time he had arrived there and finished stabling his mount, his father rode in.

'Had hoped the good weather would keep up for a few more days,' his father said as he unsaddled his horse. 'This rain will bring on those damn heel flies, and if anything makes critters spooky it's heel flies.' He spoke without looking at his son, and tended to the work of unsaddling and stalling his horse. 'You pick up many strays?'

'Some,' Thomas answered, chewing on a piece of hay. 'I chased one six-year-old twist-horn and brought him into the herd.'

William snorted. 'Sometimes it hardly pays to go after them,' he said. Then almost as though he was speaking to himself, he said, 'I generally leave them alone … I kind of feel that if they've managed to outwit us for so long, they kind of have the right to remain free.'

'A critter is a critter!' Thomas said sharply. He was annoyed with his father's attitude. The old man had strong feelings for the land and the stock on it, but practically none for men, especially his own son.

Later at dinner William told his son that he had written Clem asking him to come home early in June in order to be at the wedding. Thomas glared at his father but said nothing.

It rained all night and until close to noon of the next day. Part of the Carey herd had strayed back into the coulees and the brush to keep out of the driving rain. Some had even been stupid enough to seek protection in various arroyos and found themselves trapped by the sudden surge of water. Those that couldn't scramble free were drowned.

From the time it stopped raining until the last reddish-yellow light in the western sky faded, every hand was busy rounding up the strays, forming them into bunches, and driving the bunches to hook up with the main herd. It was hard, steady work and called for perfect coordination between the man and the cow pony.

Sometimes Thomas found a critter that was bogged down. Then he and whoever was with him would have to dig the animal out. This meant roping the cow, and while one man and his horse pulled, the other used a shovel to free the hind feet from the thick muck.

By nightfall most of the strays had been brought back to the herd and, except for the few hands who would keep watch over the stock, the men returned to the bunkhouse. Though Thomas was bone tired and dirty he took time to ride completely around the main herd to make sure that it was bedded down on a stretch of range where there were few gullies and hardly any brush. When he was satisfied, he turned his mount toward home.

He didn't mind the hard work. The fact of the matter was that he really loved it. That was why he had chosen to stay on the ranch rather than continue his schooling. Neither John nor Clem had any real feelings for raising livestock.

John, at least what Thomas could remember about him, looked a lot like his father and, though he was a good rider, spent most of his time reading. When Thomas was ten, maybe twelve, John left home. He had just turned twenty-two.

Clem followed but not the same way. Clem didn't like the ranch either but he was smart enough to put up with it until he finished his schooling in Paso Diablo. Then he convinced William to send him north to a private school. From there he went on to study law.

Three brothers, and all three of them different, almost as though they came from different parents. They looked alike except that Clem resembled his mother more than he did William.

His brothers didn't seem to possess either the physical hardness or the qualities peculiar to a rancher. But Thomas knew they were a lot smarter than he was, or at least they made their brains work rather than their bodies.

When he entered the front yard a change came over Thomas. Tired as he was, he felt the tension snake its way through his body. He shook his head. There was nothing he could do about it. The day wasn't bad. He hardly even thought about Lisa or what he would be getting into on Sunday. But once he came back to the ranch house his anger became a living thrashing thing, and when he saw his father Thomas could taste his own gall as it rose up in his throat and washed over his tongue.

Sunday came. The weather was perfect: warm with just enough of a breeze from the north to prevent it from becoming hot. The sky was bright blue with small puffs of white clouds sailing overhead like so many wind-blown bits of cotton.

After the church service, Thomas picked up his gun belt from the deacon while his father went over to congratulate the pastor on his sermon. Thomas didn't think too much about the sermon, which was about the mysterious way in which God works His wonders. It was like so many other sermons he had heard when he was a boy.

Inside the church it had been uncomfortably hot, but outside the cool breeze felt refreshing. He wondered how long his father would stand there jawing with the pastor, who now and then looked in his direction.

When he was in the church, he did not bother to look for Helen Wicker, though he knew where she was sitting because his father had pointed her out, telling him, 'There's Sam and Helen.' The very next instant the pastor had mounted the pulpit and saved him from having to make any sort of reply. But as he waited for his father, Sam and Helen came toward him.

He tipped his sombrero to Helen and greeted Sam with a hearty handshake.

'I'll pay my respects to the pastor,' Sam said and, winking broadly to Thomas, added, 'take good care of my Helen.'

Thomas nodded and for a moment his eyes followed the tall slender back of the man. Then he heaved a deep sigh and looked at Helen.

She was a small woman, slender, with hardly any breasts at all. Her eyes were light blue, her skin cream-white and there were a few freckles on the bridge of her nose. A small tuft of blonde hair escaped the confines of her bonnet.

Even as Thomas appraised her, Helen studied him. Since the last time she had seen him he had changed. Almost all the boy had been devoured by the man. And the man was tall, strong and hard — maybe even mean. Yet there was something about him that excited her. There was no doubt about it — he was good-looking, but not because his features were perfect, rather because they weren't. She had always thought there was something special about Thomas, which was why she did not object when her father suggested him as a likely prospect for a husband. Though she knew about his quick temper and the two gunfights he had had, and about the woman who worked in the Broken Horn Saloon, Helen was certain she could be a good wife to him. His reputation fascinated her. To tame him would be an accomplishment worthy of a great woman, and Helen felt equal to the challenge. Her love, together with God's blessing, would change Thomas.

'Seems to me,' she said with more southern than western drawl, 'that we should be done measuring each other.'

In spite of his feelings Thomas smiled.

'I almost thought you were fixing to draw on me.' She laughed.

'Hardly,' he answered, almost sure that she knew about his latest escapade. 'Besides, you're not wearing one of these.' And his hand dropped to his gun.

'But I am armed,' she told him, looking straight into his eyes. 'As is every woman.' Then she glanced toward the pastor and said, 'I think they're finished. Shall we go?'

He nodded and together they walked toward their respective fathers.

Sam insisted that Thomas ride in the buggy with Helen, while he rode Gray. Thomas would have protested, but a stern glance from William stopped him.

For most of the eight miles between the Wicker place and the town, neither Thomas nor Helen spoke. But as they came in sight of the house Helen said, in a very soft voice, 'Will your brother Clem be home for the wedding?'

Thomas looked at her. He felt as though he had been roped and tied, and was waiting for the searing touch of the branding iron. 'Maybe,' he answered. 'Maybe.' And he slapped the rein hard against the horse's rump to quicken the animal's pace.

Sam Wicker's place bore little resemblance to the Careys'. The house was built to resemble the southern style of architecture, complete with porticos supported by columns. There were gardens in the front and the stable was some distance from the house. Wicker had planted several oak trees when he had first built the house, and now they had grown into natural umbrellas of shade.

'Where are the slaves?' Thomas asked, as they drove up to the house.

Helen looked at him. He had asked the question to make her angry, but she wasn't about to allow him to push her into that kind of a trap. 'Some of our servants sleep in the main house,' she answered evenly, 'and the rest have their own place down by the creek.'

'Servants?' Thomas questioned.

'Servants,' she said resolutely.

Thomas did not bring up the question of the Wicker slaves throughout the rest of the afternoon, even when Sam started to run off at the mouth about the 'damn Yankee abolitionists'. As far as Thomas was concerned, he was just blowing up dust. To go to war over the question of slavery seemed almost funny. It didn't seem that any men in their right minds would want to blow each other apart. Whatever little Thomas thought about slavery made him feel that any man who owned a slave was somehow doing something wrong. But if he was, then that was his business and no one else's. On that point he would have to agree with Sam. But that was the only thing on which he agreed with him.

Finally dinner was served and everyone went into the dining room. Sam boasted that Helen had prepared every last dish that was served and Thomas had to admit that she was a 'mighty good cook'. After dinner Sam broke out some real

Cuban cigars and good southern bourbon. The talk was mostly about livestock, the condition of the range, and the coming drive to Austin. But soon the conversation swung around to the subject of the wedding.

'Did your pa tell you what Helen's dowry is?' Sam asked, looking at Thomas.

'Yes, sir.'

'I also told him,' William said, 'that he should be mighty damn thankful you're so generous.'

Sam held up his hand. 'I'm doing it for my daughter,' he said. 'And when I'm gone everything I have will belong to her.'

Thomas began to shift uneasily in his chair. It hardly seemed as though he was marrying a woman at all. He shook his head but said nothing.

Sam caught his movement and said, 'What's wrong, Thomas? If anything is bothering you, speak up.'

He felt trapped.

'Well?' William questioned.

Thomas took a deep breath and said, 'Well, sir, with all due respect —' He paused, not really having the words to express his thoughts. 'I'll be marrying your flesh and blood, and not so much land or so many critters.'

William's complexion turned a purplish red.

Sam looked at him with wide, questioning eyes. Then he smiled. 'William,' he said, still looking at Thomas, 'I think your son has just reminded me, or rather, he has reminded us, that we're not making a business deal, but we are making wedding arrangements.'

'I meant no discourtesy,' Thomas grumbled.

'But it was a point well taken,' Sam said, and proposed that they all have another drink.

The two older men toasted to the future luck and happiness of the couple, and before they drank Sam called Helen to join them, insisting that she stand by Thomas' side. 'Just as pretty as a picture,' Sam said, after he had downed his drink.

'Why don't you two young people go out for a walk,' William suggested, 'and leave us alone to talk about stock and such.'

Thomas took the opportunity to escape and offered Helen his arm. Once they were outside in the front yard and far enough away from the open windows of the dining room where what he would say would not be overheard, he stopped.

'Helen,' he said softly, 'how much do you know about this?'

She cocked her head to one side and her blonde hair slipped in front of her face, forcing her to push it back.

'I mean the marriage,' he said.

'Father asked me and I agreed,' she told him.

He raised both his hands and then in despair dropped them. 'But you don't love me,' he said. 'What's more, you don't even know me.'

She started to walk, and he quickly caught up with her.

'You come from good stock,' she told him. 'My father said that your pa was one of the bravest men he had ever seen.' She glanced at him. 'Did you know they fought together in '48?'

'Yes,' Thomas answered. 'But what they did together has nothing to do with us.'

'I grew up,' she said, stopping at the rough-hewn railing and placing her small white hands on it, 'watching you grow up. Do you remember the time I was on a big roan and he suddenly started to run?'

Thomas nodded. 'I went after you,' he said.

'You saved my life.'

'Any ranch hand would have done the same,' he told her.

'A hand might have, but not a boy of fourteen. It took a lot of courage for you to have done that.'

He wasn't going to argue that with her. Let her think what she wanted to about it. 'But you don't owe me anything,' he said.

She had her head tilted up and was looking at the blue sky. 'I never said I did,' she told him. 'But I've always remembered it.'

He shook his head. 'I'm not the marrying kind,' he said. 'At least not just yet.'

'Is it because of that saloon woman?' she asked, looking straight at him.

He could almost feel the heat of her anger. 'No,' he said, but he knew he was lying. The idea of holding this small white body against his was something he couldn't even begin to imagine. She might be pretty, and he knew lots of men who would consider her beautiful, but he would be willing to swear that she had no passion in her, no fire — at least not the kind that Lisa had.

She turned away. She saw the look on his face, and though she could not read his thoughts her female intuition told her that he had not told her the truth. Whatever hold that woman had on him was far stronger and deeper than she had dared to believe.

'You love her,' she said, still not looking at him.

'No.'

There was a ring of resoluteness in Thomas' voice that made her face him. 'You can learn to love —'

Thomas backed away.

'My love will be enough,' she said, 'for both of us.'

Again he shook his head. 'Don't you understand?' he said as gently as possible. 'Marriage isn't something that just takes place in the church.'

'It's making a home for a man,' Helen said quickly. 'A place where —'

'Yes, but there are other things,' he explained. 'Things that take place between a man and a woman.' God, how damn foolish he felt trying to tell her what her mother would have if she had lived.

'Children?' she said hopefully.

'Damn it, Helen,' he said harshly. 'I'm talking about sex — about those times when a man and a woman are naked and —'

She turned very red. 'No,' she snapped at him. 'I don't want to hear. Those things happen and they're not to be spoken of.'

She started to run but he reached out, grabbed hold of her arm and brought her close to him. 'I don't feel that way about you,' he said. 'I just don't feel that way.'

Helen took a deep breath. 'Then I'll make you,' she answered in a harsh desperate voice. 'Then I'll make you. If she can do it then so can I.'

There was more rain on Sunday night, but it wasn't bad enough to give the line riders any trouble. And by midweek the sun was bright and hot. Each day more and more critters were bunched and driven into the main herd for the branding that would follow.

Thomas worked even when his father would tell him to quit for the day and pay a 'courting call' on Helen. But he always would manage to find some reason not to go, and more often than not he would say, 'I'll wait until Sunday.'

'Suit yourself,' the old man would tell him.

'That's what I aim to do,' Thomas would answer, and then would gallop off to wherever he had to go.

The second Sunday that he and his father went out to the Wicker place Helen was much more reserved. When they were alone he asked her what was wrong.

'I had hoped you would come by during the week,' she said.

He felt guilty and told her that he had a lot of work to do.

She said she understood, but he was sure that she didn't. And by the time they finally sat down for dinner Thomas had lost whatever appetite he had. Then Sam got to spouting off about the troubles between the North and the South again.

'Sam,' he said, 'when Helen becomes my wife we ain't going to keep any slaves.'

His words stunned Sam, his father and Helen into silence. Thomas took a deep breath and said, 'I don't believe that any man should own another human being.'

He glanced at Helen. She was flushed with anger.

'That's just it!' Sam exclaimed, thumping the table with his hand. 'It's God's will to have the white man take care of the black workers..'

Thomas shook his head. 'My great-grandfather was a bondsman,' he said.

'That was different,' Sam said.

'Why?'

'He was a white man,' Sam said.

For several moments no one at the table spoke. Then Helen suggested that she and Thomas take a walk.

'Sure,' Sam said with a chuckle, 'go ahead.' And then, with a broad wink at Thomas, he added, 'I like a man who speaks his mind.'

Thomas nodded and, with Helen at his side, left the dining room. 'Do you really feel that way about Negroes?' Helen asked when they had reached the shade of the oak trees, 'or were you just trying to rile my father?'

Thomas shrugged. 'About half and half,' he said.

'At least you're honest,' she told him.

'How do *you* feel about them?' he asked.

'If you don't want any slaves,' Helen said, looking up at him, 'we won't have any. Does that answer your question?'

It didn't, but he nodded, hoping that they would drop the subject.

'Let's walk a bit,' Helen said, and she took hold of his hand.

They went beyond the fence and out on to the open plain. The recent rain and the hot sun had done its work, and the earth was covered with new light-green grass. They walked to the top of a small rise and went down the other side. Then Helen stopped. She looked around and said, 'It almost seems as if we're the only two people alive. I can't even see the top of the house from here.' She faced him and asked, 'Does it seem that way when you're alone … I mean when you're riding the range?'

'More so,' he answered.

She lowered herself and sat down on the grass. 'Sit down next to me,' she said, looking up at him.

Thomas sat down.

'When I was a little girl,' she told him, 'I would come out here, stretch out, and look up at the sky to look at the clouds.'

He didn't answer.

'What did you do?' she asked.

'I learned to ride, rope and shoot.'

Helen lay back and stretched her arms over her head. 'I can see a cloud that looks like some sort of an animal,' she told him.

He looked up at the sky.

'You can't see it that way,' she chided. 'You have to look at it from down here.'

Thomas suddenly realized what she was trying to do. 'I think we should be getting back,' he said, starting to get to his feet.

Helen caught hold of his hand.

He looked down at her and saw that her eyes were lidded and her small breasts rapidly rose and fell. The next instant he bent over her.

'I love you, Thomas,' she whispered, circling his neck with her arms and drawing him to her. 'I love you.'

His lips pressed hers. The scent of lilac sachet and crushed grass filled his head. Her body trembled as his kiss became more passionate. But it was not a passion born out of love. It came because she was a woman. There was nothing more to it.

Thomas tried to draw away. But she held him fast, with a strength that belied her frail body.

'I wanted you to kiss me so very much,' she whispered. 'Oh, Thomas, I know I can make you happy.'

He knew that if he wanted her she would have let him take her. But even as this realization played like a cat with a mouse in the recesses of his brain he sensed they were not alone. He looked up. On the crest of the hill were two giggling Children, too young to fully understand what they saw but old enough to guess.

He pulled himself away from Helen. The mood had vanished just as quickly as the children had taken to their heels as soon as they saw him looking at them.

'What's wrong?' she asked.

'Nothing!' he exclaimed, getting to his feet. He reached down and offered her his hand. 'We best be getting back.'

She nodded and stood up. Neither of them said anything during the long walk back to the house.

FIVE

The roundup ended by the middle of the week, then the branding began. It was slow, hard work, especially since the heel flies relentlessly tormented the critters. Thomas did more than his share of roping, bringing the unmarked calves to the flankers, who in turn downed the animals for the brander.

The air was filled with the stench of singed hair and burnt hide. Mr Cowper, his father's top hand, kept count of the number of calves marked with the WC brand. There were thousands of them. Once a calf was branded he was turned loose and went bawling back to his mother.

One evening during the week Thomas took off to visit Helen. He didn't want any more recriminations from her. And then Saturday night came. Most of the hands were going into Paso Diablo, and Rusty asked him to join them.

'No thanks,' he said. 'I'll just stick around the ranch.'

All of the men knew he was soon to be married to Sam Wicker's daughter, and a few of them laughed and kidded him about 'puttin' his brand on Sam's blonde filly'. He took their comments good-naturedly, but stood fast to his decision not to go to Paso Diablo. He spent the better part of the evening playing stud poker with those hands who remained. His mind wasn't on the game, and by the time he quit he had lost more than he had won.

Before Thomas left the bunkhouse he rolled a cigarette and lit it. Then he went out into the cool spring night. The moon was already in its last phase and the yellow crescent seemed to be resting on the low top of the distant mountains. He walked slowly. In a little more than a month he'd be a married man. Each time he saw Helen this became more of a reality.

He stopped and looked in the direction of Paso Diablo, then suddenly he made up his mind and went to the stable. A few minutes later he saddled Gray and rode out of the front yard. He didn't push Gray, but nonetheless the animal broke into a trot. Just before he reached the town he swung off the road and made his way to the knoll overlooking the town, where he reined Gray to a halt.

Thomas knew that he should not be going into town, and though he tried to convince himself that he would only stop for a few drinks at the Broken Horn, he couldn't lie to himself. He desperately wanted to see Lisa— not only see her, but be with her the way he had so often been. He wanted to feel the touch of her naked breasts against his bare chest. He wanted to feel her body under his.

He gripped the saddle's horn with such force that his fingers ached. If he did go, more than likely he'd find her with someone else, and then he'd feel like seven kinds of a fool again. Besides, there was Helen to think about. She would find out about his visit even if he never mentioned it.

He eased his hold on the horn. He owed Helen something if for no other reason than her love for him. Since that first Sunday when he and his father went to the Wicker place for dinner, Thomas had spent a good deal of his time thinking about her, though not the way he thought about Lisa.

Lisa was part of him the way a river was part of the land through which it flowed. It gave to the land and at the same time it took from the land. Lisa was like that. But Helen was different. Slender as she was, her strength was rock hard. He knew that he could build on it, and that she would be able to withstand everything and anything the future had to offer and still stay at his side.

He didn't love her, but he had come to respect her. He even respected her willingness to give herself to him if that would have made him happy. 'She has spunk,' he said aloud. 'There's no denying that.'

Gray heard his voice and his head instantly bobbed up.

'Maybe she's right,' he told his mount. 'Maybe she has enough love in her for the two of us.'

He wheeled Gray around to the left, rode back down the knoll to the road, and was about to head back to the ranch when the familiar sounds of the night were torn apart by the sharp, decisive explosions of gunfire. The sound brought him up sharply, and he halted Gray. From the way the echoes bounced across the plain Thomas knew that they had been fired outside. He swung his mount around and rode for Paso Diablo at a gallop.

Just as he entered the main street a band of riders moved slowly toward him. Thomas drew off to the side and brought Gray to a halt in the shadow of the first building on the street. His right hand dropped to his gun. Even before the men reached him he saw that one horse had the body of a man slung over it.

It was too dark for him.to recognize any one of the men until they were just a few yards in front of him. And then he saw Mr Cowper. His eyes picked out the other hands, all except Rusty, and he knew who was slung across the saddle.

'Mister Cowper,' he called, easing Gray out of the shadow of the building and into the middle of the street.

The man drew his mount to a halt. The others reined in too.

'What happened?' Thomas asked, ignoring the man's questioning look.

'One of Johnson's hands gunned down Rusty,' he answered.

Rusty had ridden for his father for three, maybe four years. Thomas had never known him to start trouble.

'Why?' he asked.

Cowper shrugged. 'Jest some of Johnson's hands on the prod.'

Thomas knew there was more to it than that. But he couldn't force Cowper to talk if he didn't want to.

'Didn't think you were comin' in,' Cowper said.

'I wasn't,' Thomas said. 'I got as far as the knoll there.' He gestured to the rise above the town. 'I was heading back to the ranch when I heard the shots.'

'Best you come back with us,' Cowper said. 'Johnson's hands are still in the Broken Horn.'

'Who shot Rusty?'

'Don't know his name,' Cowper said.

'Aron,' one of the other hands said.

Cowper shrugged. 'Rusty was playin' poker at one of the tables and this weaselly-lookin' guy accuses him of cheatin'. The next thing I heard was this weaselly guy callin' Rusty out.' He shook his head sadly. 'Rusty wouldn't know how to cheat at cards or anythin' else,' he said.

The other men voiced their agreement with Cowper and then one said, 'Rusty was no match for a good hand with a gun. He never got his clear of the holster.'

'That's a fact,' Cowper attested. 'Rusty's gun never cleared.' He glanced back at the body slung over the saddle. 'Sure don't seem right,' he said, 'but it's done with.'

'You take the men back to the ranch,' Thomas said.

'You're a fool if you're goin' to do what I think —'

'Rusty wasn't cheating,' Thomas told them.

The men murmured their agreement.

'He was gunned down because of —' He stopped. Then in a much lower voice he said, 'Because of me. The man I shot was his friend. I owe Rusty, and I'm not one who doesn't pay what he owes.'

The men were silent for a few moments. Then Cowper said, 'Don't think Rusty will mind none if we spend a bit more time in town.'

'It's not your fight,' Thomas said.

'Maybe not,' the top hand said. 'But you're one man. Besides that weaselly-looking man there are maybe eight or ten more of Johnson's riders there. Seems to me like you might want them to stay put for a spell — at least till you and that Aron fellow had the chance to get things straightened out.'

Thomas nodded, and he and the other hands rode slowly up the street of Paso Diablo. When they reached the Broken Horn Saloon they secured their horses to the hitching post and slipped their guns free of the holsters. They entered the Broken Horn Saloon. They moved quickly, fanning out in the shadow of the wall so that the men at the bar, and those at the tables, would not be able to move without being seen by them.

Thomas stood at the swinging door and quickly found the table where Aron sat. Zeb was there too.

He took three large steps away from the door and stopped. His right hand hung above his gun. Out of the corner of his eye he saw Tiny move to the far side of the bar. He hoped that the barkeep wouldn't go for the gun he kept under the bar. But if he did, Thomas knew that one of his own men would cut him down.

He took a moment longer to look for Lisa. She was nowhere in sight. The sure knowledge that she was upstairs with one of Johnson's hands made him bite his lip.

'Aron,' he called. 'You gunned down the wrong man!'

His deadly calm voice snapped out like a bull whip. Instantly the men started to move.

'Stay where you are,' he ordered. 'Every man jack of you is covered.'

All movement stopped. A moment passed.

'He's bluffing,' Zeb said, starting to move.

A shot rang out and slammed into the floor in front of Zeb. The man fell back into has chair and almost tipped it over.

'Aron?' Thomas called again.

'It was a fair —'

'I won't wait much longer,' Thomas said.

Very slowly, the man stood up.

'That's right,' Thomas said. 'Now all you have to do is walk outside.'

'I have no quarrel with you,' the man whined.

'Step away from the table,' Thomas told him.

Aron hesitated and cast a quick glance at Zeb.

'Make a move,' Thomas warned, 'and you're a dead man.'

Zeb remained motionless.

Aron moved clear of the table and started toward Thomas, who gestured him forward with his left hand.

Slowly Thomas backed away, and when his back reached the swinging doors he told his men to shoot any man who moved.

After what seemed like hours he had Aron in the street. Sweat covered his brow and ran down his cheeks.

'All right, little man,' Thomas said, 'I'm going to give you the same chance you gave Rusty. Now make your play!'

'I ain't no match for you,' Aron complained.

'Rusty wasn't a match for you, but that didn't seem to bother you none. Make your play.'

The sheriff came running down the street. He ordered Thomas to put up his gun.

'This is none of your affair, Mr Wyler,' he said. 'Keep out of it!'

'I warned you the last time,' the sheriff said.

'He killed one of my hands.'

Wyler turned toward Aron and saw him draw. 'Good God!' he exclaimed, realizing the man had taken advantage of the situation.

An instant later a single shot rang out. The man staggered backwards and fell to his knees clutching his chest, then dropped face downward into the dirt of the main street.

The sheriff turned to Thomas. It was too dark to see the smoke from his gun, but Wyler knew it was there. He shook his head. There was nothing he could say.

William was a light sleeper, and when Thomas rode Gray out of the front yard he was awake and at the window before his son had passed through the gate. His first impulse was to call him back, but as the distance between Thomas and the ranch widened, he started to dress so that he could go after him.

As soon as William was fully clothed he changed his mind. It didn't seem proper for him to be chasing after a grown man. Besides, if he caught up with Thomas he was sure they would argue.

William looked at his crumpled bed. Even if he did go back to it, he knew he wouldn't be able to sleep, at least not until Thomas returned. He walked out into the main room, lit an oil lamp and then went for the Bible. He opened it again to the story of the Prodigal Son and started to read, but soon found that he couldn't. He set the book back on the shelf and, opening the door, looked out into the night.

For more days than he cared to remember, he had watched his son become more and more taut. Whenever he had tried to speak to him, Thomas had kept a tight rein on his words. And in the past few days Thomas had kept silent even when they sat down to dinner. This was a hard thing for William to bear. Though William never said it in so many words, he loved Thomas more than his other boys. Maybe that was because with all his shenanigans Thomas was the only one of his sons who loved the land.

William knew what was tearing at his son, but he was equally sure that once Thomas was married, Helen would be able to make him forget that woman in Paso Diablo. The boy would come to his senses and see where his responsibility lay.

In his time he remembered that he had sown some wild oats too, and his father had done the same thing before him. Ethan his father, had — Passionate blood had always flowed through the veins of Carey men. It was their strength and their weakness.

William was living proof of his father's weakness. He was born out of wedlock and given to Ethan's wife to raise. And when William discovered he was a bastard he could not stand the sight of Ethan, or the woman who was his father's wife. He hated them! This hate had destroyed the family.

William had seen it all happen. He had been a party to the happening. He began to fear that Thomas would repeat Ethan's mistakes.

William would do anything to prevent a repetition of that past agony even if it meant losing Thomas.

He shook his head and silently prayed that Thomas too would find God and thus the strength to resist temptation. He went inside for his pipe, only to return to the open door when the tobacco was lit. Impatiently he waited for his son to return.

The hours passed with a terrible slowness. He watched the thin moon disappear from the night sky and marked the changing position of the familiar constellations. His sense of foreboding grew as the stars in the east began to dim with the coming of the first light of day. Just as the gray of dawn washed over the land he saw the men and their horses cresting the rise some distance from the house. He left the doorway and walked slowly to the middle of the front yard, where he stopped and waited.

From the slack way the men sat in their saddles William guessed that something was wrong. His heart began to beat faster and his throat suddenly felt very dry. There were eight horses, but he could only see seven men.

The next instant he caught sight of the limp mass slung over one of the saddles.

'Oh, my God!' he whispered aloud. He started to move, but immediately checked himself and remained where he was.

Several minutes passed, but the half-light prevented him from recognizing either a particular man or his mount. One rider moved up from the rear and came ahead of the others. In a matter of moments he knew it was his son. He coughed to clear his throat.

Once Thomas was inside the fence he halted Gray and dismounted. He looked at his father and then glanced back at the other riders, who were still a few yards behind him. He heard Mr Cowper tell the other hands to ride on to the bunkhouse and that he'd be along shortly. Then he came up to Thomas and swung out of the saddle.

'There's no need for you to come,' Thomas told him.

'Your pa might not understand how it was,' Cowper answered.

Thomas shrugged, took Gray's reins and led him toward his old man. When he was in front of him he stopped and said, 'Rusty was gunned down by one of Johnson's hands.'

William said nothing.

'Claimed he was cheating at cards,' Thomas explained.

The old man still remained silent.

'Begging your pardon, Mr Carey,' Cowper began, 'but Thomas here is a right brave man.'

William's eyes flicked over to his top hand and then went back to his son. 'You just had to go,' he said slowly. 'You couldn't keep away from that whore.'

'I didn't even see her,' Thomas answered defensively. 'I didn't intend to go into town, leastways not until I heard the shooting.'

His father snorted with disbelief.

'I went as far as the knoll outside of Paso Diablo.'

Cowper cut in and explained how Rusty had been shot. 'And then,' he said, 'Thomas came along.'

William looked at his son.

'I called the bastard out,' Thomas told him. 'It was a fair fight. Ask Sheriff Wyler.'

'You killed him.'

'One shot,' Cowper said. 'Hit him in the chest.'

'And now what?' William asked, his eyes narrowed to slits and fixed on Thomas. 'Tell me now what?'

'I did what I had to do,' Thomas said sullenly.

'And you think that it will rest there, do you?' William questioned harshly. 'Killing begets killing. That's two of Johnson's men you've put into their graves. Don't you think some of his hands might think they have a score to settle with you?' He shook his head. 'The trouble with you,' he told his son, 'is that you enjoy killing.'

'No.'

'Your actions speak louder than your words,' his father said. 'Haven't we got enough trouble with Johnson coming here and taking cattle from our range land?'

'It wasn't his fault,' Cowper said. 'Rusty was a good man and a friend of his.'

'The man who killed Rusty was with the other one I shot,' Thomas explained. 'He had no cause to shoot him. He did it because of me.'

'And how many more of our hands will be killed because of you?'

'None,' Thomas snapped. 'The fight's over. There's only one of them left, and Zeb has a long wide yellow streak running down his back.'

William squinted at him. 'You're a fool,' he said in a hard voice. And then he turned his attention to Cowper. 'Tell the men I'll bring the pastor back with me after church to read over Rusty.'

'Yes, Mr Carey,' the top hand answered.

'And you can also tell them we're going to start the drive early this year.' Then he turned and went back into the house.

'You shouldn't have stood up for me,' Thomas said to Cowper as soon as his father was in the house.

'I reckon I has to just the way you had to call that man out.'

A thin smile formed on Thomas' lips. 'My pa don't think so,' he said.

The top hand shrugged. 'He ain't the easiest man to get on with, but he's fair and honest,' he said. 'And that's about all any man can ask of another.'

'Thanks,' Thomas answered.

'Deep down in his gut,' Cowper commented, 'your pa — well, damn it, you know how he feels.'

Thomas nodded, and the top hand turned his mount around and walked him slowly toward the bunkhouse.

Thomas watched for several moments, then guided Gray to the stable. He did know how his father felt, and it wasn't at all the way Cowper thought. The old man was harder than anyone thought he was. And he had damn little use for his youngest son! Well, the feeling was mutual — or was it?

Thomas could never get himself to say that he hated his father. He couldn't even think it. He recognized they were different and allowed for the difference, which was a helluva lot more than his old man did.

What the hell — thinking about it wasn't going to change him, or his father.

SIX

On Sunday Helen and her father were supposed to go to the Carey ranch for dinner, but all that was changed when they found out about Rusty's death. They still came out to the ranch, but they were just part of the many hands and ranchers who had known Rusty and who thought it proper to pay their last respects.

William had Maria busy in the kitchen preparing food for all the people who had come to Rusty's funeral. And Sam sent one of his men back to his place for his cook and a couple of the women to help with the serving.

The pastor said a few words about Rusty, and then admitted that he didn't know the man too well since Rusty was not a churchgoer. 'But,' he said in his deep voice, 'I am told by Mister Carey that the man we are about to commit to his untimely grave was honest, hard-working and, by the number of the mourners here, I judge, he was well liked.'

A murmur of approval arose from the men clustered around the grave.

Then the pastor asked everyone to join him in the saying of the Twenty-third Psalm. As soon as he started, the men and women joined in. Their collective voice rose above the sound of the wind blowing across the plain. When it was over he nodded, and the four men holding the sling ropes began to lower the plain raw wood coffin into the six-by-six hole.

The ladies wept as they watched the men pay out the ropes. As soon as the box was down and the ropes pulled clear, William stepped up to the mound of earth, picked up the shovel and dropped the dirt into the grave, filling it. Thomas followed him, and then Cowper. The rest of the hands took their turn until the grave was filled and a mound of raw earth grew over it. Finally a wooden cross was hammered into place at the head of the grave. Rusty's name was painted on it, followed by the words REST IN PEACE.

As soon as the marker was set everyone turned and headed back to the ranch house, where tables were already laid out with food and drink. Thomas did not move from the graveside. The grave and the marker seemed damn little for a man to have at the end of his life. Of all the men who rode for his father, with the exception of Cowper, he had liked Rusty the best. Probably because the man was a good hand and didn't have to palaver all of the time, the way some men did.

'Didn't anyone know how old he was?' someone asked in a small voice.

He turned and saw Helen.

'Reckon not,' he answered, with a shake of his head. 'But maybe he was as old as I am, give or take a year or two.'

'I'm sorry,' she said, knowing that Thomas must have liked the man if he had remained at the grave.

'Like the pastor said,' he told her, 'the Lord giveth and the Lord taketh away.'

'Blessed be the name of the Lord,' Helen said, finishing the sentence for him.

Thomas walked to the head of the grave and ran his hand over the marker. 'I evened the score, Rusty,' he commented, and then he looked at Helen. 'I guess we should join the others.'

She went around to where he stood. 'Not if you don't want to,' she said, looking up at his tightly drawn face.

'We'll be missed.'

She shrugged and, reaching for his hand, said, 'Let's walk.'

Hand in hand they left the graveside and began to walk. Neither one spoke. From time to time Thomas glanced up at the blue cloudless sky. It was very blue and very bright — the kind of sky that was too beautiful to be real.

'Thomas,' Helen said, breaking the silence between them, 'I have something to ask you.'

He faced her.

'I know this may not be the right time,' she told him, 'but I must know.'

'What?'

'Did you go to Paso Diablo last night to see —'

He stopped so abruptly that Helen stumbled and he had to grab hold of her to stop her from falling. They stood face to face, so close that her breasts touched his chest. And he could feel their softness with each breath she took.

'I started to,' he said, 'but I didn't.' And he explained what had happened.

Her blue eyes suddenly seemed bluer and much, much brighter.

'What made you change your mind?'

'I just did,' he said, knowing that she wanted a different answer, one that he couldn't give.

The light in her eyes dimmed, and she could not keep the disappointment from her face. 'I had hoped,' she told him in a choked voice, 'that maybe your feelings for me had something to do with it.'

He remained silent.

'Well,' she said, 'at least you did change your mind.' And with a hint of a sob in her voice she added, 'I guess I'll have to be content with that.'

'I guess so,' he answered, and reached down to take hold of her hand.

'No!' she exclaimed, jerking her hand away from his. 'I wouldn't want you to —'

She turned and ran from him. It took Thomas a few moments to realize what had happened, but as soon as he did he went after her. 'Listen,' he said, as soon as he caught up with her, 'running away from me won't change matters.'

'You're impossible!' she shouted at him. 'Just impossible!' And the next moment she rushed at him, beating his chest with her small balled fists.

He grabbed hold of her wrists. 'Don't you ever do that again,' he said threateningly as she struggled to free herself. Then suddenly Helen went limp. Thomas let go of her hands. In an instant something had happened, a change had occurred. Both of them were breathing hard.

Never had he seen Helen so beautiful, so full of wild fury! He was stirred by it.

She too sensed the change. She saw it in the way he was looking at her and she moved closer to him. Helen closed her eyes and lifted her face. She felt his lips come down on hers in a hot, moist kiss. Her body quivered with a strange, delicious excitement. His hands moved over her back and then she felt his fingers fumble with the small buttons on the front of her bodice.

Helen couldn't move away and she was too terrified to tell him to stop.

He thrust his hand into her open dress and down the top of her shift until he held her small warm breast.

'Do you love me?' she asked in a quivering voice.

'I want you!' he said harshly, emphasizing the answer he gave by rubbing his hand over her breast.

'But what if someone —'

He silenced her objections with a kiss and together they sank down into the rich green grass. He pushed the long hem of her dress up and reached under her shift until he touched her womanhood.

She closed her eyes and felt his weight on her. And when he finally thrust his body against hers she gasped from the sudden stab of pain.

The moments rushed by, and then it was over.

Oblivious to what was happening to Helen, Thomas quickened his movements, and when the fluid of his passion finally burst free, he gave a low, throaty growl of pleasure. And then he rolled off her. His need had been satisfied.

Helen opened her eyes and looked into the dazzling blue of the sky. Her body hurt, but it was worth it. She had given him what he wanted. Maybe now he would understand how much she loved him.

Thomas stared up at the cloudless sky, vaguely aware of the woman who had just given him her virginity, but oddly conscious of the strange connection between passion and death. He didn't love Helen, yet he had wanted her. He wondered why.

'Are you sorry?' she asked after several minutes had passed.

He rolled his head toward her. 'We'll be married as soon as I come back from the drive,' he answered.

Helen smiled and nodded. 'You see,' she whispered, 'I can make you happy too.'

He didn't answer; he turned his head back toward the sky. Silently he whispered Lisa's name over and over again.

SEVEN

The drive began at sunup on Wednesday. Two dozen drovers began to move the herd until the three thousand head formed up into a long column strung out about a mile from end to end.

Thomas rode point with Bill Herrick, the top hand from Sam Wicker's ranch. Herrick was a chunkily built, dark-complexioned man, and had a reputation for being a hard driver. He was a few years older than Thomas, and from what little was known about him, he had been born in Tennessee.

William was trail boss and Mr Cowper was his *secundo*. Those drovers who rode the flank, swing, or drag positions came from the half-dozen ranches whose stock made up the herd. The wranglers for the remuda were all Mex vaqueros, hired for the job. Two chuck wagons followed the herd until it was formed up, and then they moved to a place on the flanks.

The first two days on the trail were hard on the men as well as the animals. The drovers pressed the herd to cover as much ground as possible in order to get them away from familiar range land, and to tire them out so that they would have less trouble bedding them down at night. The swing and flank riders had their hands full keeping the balky critters from straying out of the line of march.

But by the third day the herd had organized itself. The strongest steers took up the lead and the others followed. The twist-horn that Thomas had run out of the arroyo during the roundup was up front in the lead position.

Though the drive moved well and the good weather held, there was an unmistakable pall over the drive. Thomas had been on enough drives to sense the feeling of the men. He guessed that Rusty's death had something to do with the general uneasiness. And of course every man wondered what Johnson might try once he found out that they had gotten the jump on him.

Any gunplay near the herd would send it on a wild stampede, which could easily not only cost their head start, but could very well cause any one of them to be maimed for life or to be smashed to a lifeless mass by the running cattle.

But Thomas didn't fret over either possibility. He took each day as it came and enjoyed riding point, which usually kept him several miles ahead of the herd. Now and then he'd join up with Herrick and for a while they would ride together.

Herrick wasn't much of a talker, but Thomas soon realized that Herrick's lack of talk wasn't the same as Rusty's. Rusty was a naturally silent man, whereas Herrick was silent only when he was with him; otherwise he seemed to do a lot of talking, especially at night to the other drovers from Sam's place.

Thomas figured the man had more to say to his friends than he had to him. It didn't bother him none as long as he did his job. A man was free to talk to whomever he pleased.

The only time Thomas got to see his father was at night, and then neither of them wasted words, exchanging comments only about those things that concerned the next day's ride. Thomas preferred it that way. The one thing he didn't want was to have his father constantly peck away at what had happened. To avoid any argument between them, he didn't even ask why they were going to Corpus Christi instead of San Antonio or Austin, which was where they had driven the herd in past years. Even if he had asked, Thomas knew that the old man would not answer unless he wanted to. A long time ago he had learned that his father would say nothing at all until he was ready.

Late in the afternoon on the fifth day, large flat-bottomed clouds gathered in the north and quickly grew into immense thunderheads that looked like huge ships with all sails spread. Thomas reined in his mount and studied the clouds. The sun was still hot, but the air was considerably more humid than it had been.

'Looks like a storm is building,' Thomas called out to Herrick, who was some distance off to his right and slightly behind him.

'Don't see that it matters much,' the other rider answered.

Thomas gestured to him, and a few moments later Herrick drew up to him and halted.

'There's the smell of rain,' Thomas noted. Then, pointing in front of them, he said, 'The trail dips off into a wash there. If we got hit with a thunderstorm it might be tricky work getting the herd across it.'

'You ain't worried about a little shower, are you?' Herrick asked.

Thomas didn't like the question, or the way the man asked it.

'I don't guess it's more than three o'clock,' Herrick told him. 'The herd could be on the far side of that wash in a couple of hours.'

Thomas nodded his agreement and then said, 'But I don't think that rain will hold off.'

'Then you ride back and tell your pa that you think he should play it close to the vest.' This time Herrick didn't even try to make the tone of his voice sound civil. 'But tell him it was your idea. I'm for pushing on.'

'I'll tell him,' Thomas said, as he started to wheel his mount around.

'You should learn not to scare so easily,' Herrick commented.

Thomas stopped his turn. 'All right,' he said. 'We had better settle whatever is bothering you right now.' His blood began to race with anger. The man was needling him and he didn't know why.

Herrick looked at him with steely eyes. Then he started to turn his mount away.

Thomas dropped the reins and grabbed hold of the bridle with his left hand, forcing Herrick's mount to turn back. 'You have something to say, you better say it straight out,' he told the man.

'Let go of it,' Herrick said sharply, 'or I'll blow your hand off.'

Thomas saw him go for his gun. Instinctively he went for his own, then changed his mind and released the bridle.

Herrick's lips formed into a thin smile. 'Didn't think you wanted to go all the way to a showdown,' he said. 'At least not when the odds aren't stacked in your favor. Now why don't you turn around like a good boy and go tell your daddy —'

'We'll settle this another time,' Thomas said angrily.

'Any time, boy,' Herrick answered, and swung away.

Filled with impotent anger, Thomas wheeled around and spurred his mount into a gallop back toward the herd. He didn't understand why Herrick had tried to provoke him. He hardly knew the man. Had it come to a showdown between them, Thomas didn't doubt that he would have killed him.

By the time he came in sight of the herd, he slowed his mount to a quick trot and swung toward the boss wagon where his father usually rode when he wasn't in the saddle.

'To spend a horse like that,' William said, as his son came alongside of the wagon, 'a man must be crazy. Or have something very important to say.'

'There's a storm building up,' Thomas said, looking up at his father.

'Is that what made you ride like ten devils were after you?'

'The trail dips down into a wash a couple of miles from here.'

William leaned over the side of the wagon and studied the clouds. They formed into a towering wall that had grown considerably darker and more ominous than when Cowper had called his attention to them. 'How far across the wash?' he asked.

'Give or take a bit, about a mile,' Thomas answered. 'I don't think we should try to cross it.'

'What about Herrick?' his father questioned. 'What does he think?'

'We should push on,' Thomas replied sullenly. He was almost sure that the old man would continue, just to go contrary to his suggestion.

William swung off the highboard of the wagon and on to his mount, which had been tethered to the side of the wagon. 'Ride back to Herrick,' he said, 'and tell him we'll bed down for the night. When that storm breaks, we'll have enough trouble trying to keep the herd together.'

'I'll send another drover,' Thomas said.

'So that's the way it is,' William said. 'I was wondering how long it would take you to get into trouble.'

Thomas glared at him. 'God damn it!' he exclaimed. 'Must you always be my judge and jury?'

'So help me God,' William shot back at him, 'if you start anything with any of the men, I'll whip the hide off you.' And then he rode off to find Cowper.

It didn't take the drovers long to bunch the cattle together for the night. They too had been watching the clouds and were wondering whether it might not be better to call a halt for the day. By the time the men had finished rounding up the strays, the wind had become much stronger and considerably colder. A few of the men remained with the herd to father it, until they were relieved by the first guard shift.

Thomas left the boss wagon and rode over to the remuda, where he exchanged his pony for another one from his string. Then he went back to the boss wagon and watched the herd being bedded down.

In a little while Herrick, and the drover sent to fetch him, came riding into camp. Thomas looked straight at Herrick, and he stared back. Neither man would give the other the satisfaction of looking away, but eventually Herrick swung away to join the small group around Sam's cook wagon.

By the time William returned to the boss wagon, the sky was completely clouded over and the low mumble of thunder rolled across the plain. The rain came on a sudden gust of wind. Anything that wasn't tied down blew away. In a matter of moments the men were drenched, and then came the blazing streaks of lightning that changed the darkness into an eerie kind of light. The first crash of thunder seemed to shake the ground. Explosion after explosion followed each jagged streak of lightning. Then someone shouted, 'Boys, the cattle is runnin'!'

That was enough to send every man to his horse.

Thomas found himself riding hard near Cowper, the two of them trying to work their way in front of a running stream of fear-crazed steers in order to turn them and bring them to a halt. They raced the steers, yelling at them and waving their slickers in front of them.

'Turn, you bastards, turn!' Thomas shouted above the din of pounding hooves and the crash of thunder. His throat ached and his arms felt leaden, but he continued to shout and flail his slicker. Suddenly the critters turned back to the tight circle of the herd. But somehow a few would always manage to swing out, and then he or Cowper would ride after them and the chase would begin over again.

Finally the thunder and lightning passed, and only a cold hard downpour remained. The herd was easier to control, but it was too worked up to be bedded down again. All the men could do was to ride around it and prevent any more of the critters from straying.

Thomas and Cowper were on the far side of the herd. They had worked together, and now that the cattle had stopped running and were just milling about they moved closer to each other.

'Think we lost many?' Cowper asked, keeping his voice very low lest the sound of it should spook the nervous cattle.

'Hard to tell,' Thomas whispered. 'We seemed to have turned them before they really started to run.'

'Your pa mentioned the wash up ahead,' Cowper said. 'We'd sure be in a mess if we were caught there.'

Thomas didn't answer.

'I once saw a herd get caught in something like that during a rainstorm, and less than half of it got out,' Cowper continued. 'That wash filled up with water so fast that it was just sheer luck any stock got out of it.'

'Well, at least that didn't happen.'

'Your pa said that Herrick was for pushin' on,' Cowper said.

'I guess he figured we could have crossed it before the storm hit.'

'He's a good hand,' Cowper commented.

'I didn't say he wasn't,' Thomas answered, wiping the rain from his face. 'Sam wouldn't have him if he weren't.'

'I told your pa to give him his wages and send him back,' Cowper said.

'But why —?'

'Keep your voice down!' Cowper warned. 'Or we'll be chasing these damn critters till sunup.'

'You just told me he was a good hand,' Thomas said, lowering his voice to a whisper again.

'He is,' Cowper affirmed. 'And a good hand doesn't push ahead across a wash with a thunderstorm on the loose. Your pa said you had words with him. Not that it's any of my business,' Cowper told him, 'but I heard some of the other drovers talking about Herrick. Seems like he's kind of pissed that you're going to marry Sam's daughter.'

'What?' Thomas questioned, almost standing in his stirrups. He immediately wondered if Helen had known. And then he realized that even if she had, it would not have changed his situation.

'The way I heard it,' Cowper explained, 'he was fixin' to ask her to marry him when you started to court her. But I thought you knowed that.'

'No,' Thomas said. 'I didn't know it.'

'Now you understand why I told your pa to pay 'im back?'

'Yes,' Thomas answered. And without saying anything more to Cowper he rode a little way off from him and stopped.

He needed to be alone for a while, and as he sat hunched over in his saddle with the cold rain beating down on him, he felt sorry for Herrick. They had more in common than the other man would ever believe, and Thomas was almost happy that he hadn't drawn his gun. But he also knew that sending him away wouldn't be the end of it, not if Herrick was the kind of man he seemed to be. If the man needed killing, Thomas hoped he wouldn't have to be the one to do it.

After the stampede the drive seemed to go better than before. It was almost as if the men had undergone a kind of baptism of fire, and during it had discovered a source of confidence in themselves that had remained hidden until the critters had gone on a rampage.

Thomas soon found out that Herrick had been stirring up the men, telling them dire stories about what Johnson intended to do if he caught up with the herd. Herrick also mentioned that he had heard from one of Johnson's men, the last time he had been in Paso Diablo, that Zeb was going after the man who had gunned down his brother and his friend.

This information came to Thomas in bits and pieces from what the various drovers let pass their lips, either accidentally or to put him on notice about Zeb and Herrick.

What Thomas learned he kept to himself. There was no reason, the way he figured, to say anything about it to his father or Cowper. If trouble came from either Zeb or Herrick it would be his, and he would not involve any of the other drovers or his father, who had enough to worry about with Johnson.

The rest of the time on the trail passed without incident. Johnson didn't show up to hobble their progress or, worse, scatter the herd. And if Zeb had intended to have a showdown with Thomas, he must have changed his mind.

Twenty-two days after the drive began, William ordered a halt just a few miles outside Corpus Christi. He planned to bring the herd into the city early the following morning and sell it off by noon. He eased himself off the boss wagon and went about the routine of making camp for the night.

By the time Thomas had come in from riding point, the herd was already bedded down. Off in the distance a drover was singing to keep the critters steady. His voice carried a long, long distance.

Thomas tethered his mount to the side of the boss wagon and paused for a few moments to listen to the singing before unsaddling. The words were in Spanish and he understood them. The song was about a young vaquero in love with a beautiful *señorita* who was too proud and heartless to even look at the man.

'Sounds kind of pretty,' his father said, looking up at him. He was seated on the top of an empty box toward the rear of the wagon, drinking a cup of strong black coffee.

Thomas glanced at him and nodded. Even after Herrick had left, Thomas' conversations with the old man hadn't changed much. But the more he thought about it the more Thomas realized that by sending Herrick back the old man had, so to speak, stepped between them. He didn't want or need his father's protection, and he felt the old man had no right to interfere.

The singing stopped and Thomas began to unsaddle the horse.

'Leave that be,' William said, 'and come have some coffee.'

Thomas hesitated.

'It's all right,' William told him, 'you can tend to him later.'

Thomas shrugged, walked to where his father sat and hunkered down next to him.

The old man lifted the coffee pot from the fire, poured some into the cup and handed it to his son. 'Go ahead and drink,' he said.

Thomas took the cup, thanked him, and drank.

William studied him. The days on the trail had darkened the boy's complexion even more than it had been before the drive. 'Seems like all my worrying about Johnson was for nothing,' he said, turning to look into the fire.

'Seems that way,' Thomas answered, passing the empty cup back to his father.

'Want some more?'

'I had enough,' he said.

William poured coffee into the cup and began to sip it. Then he said, 'I'm not planning to spend more time in Christi than necessary.' He turned his face toward his son and looked at him questioningly.

'No more than is necessary for me to get a bath and maybe buy a few things,' Thomas answered.

William nodded and went back to drinking his coffee. After a while he asked, 'You planning to bring a present back for Helen?'

Thomas hadn't thought about buying anything for her and didn't see why he should. But rather than rile his father, he said, 'If I see something that catches my fancy and I think she might like it.'

The old man smiled. 'She's a really pretty woman,' he commented. 'Sometimes I wonder why some other young fellow didn't —'

'Herrick wanted to marry her,' Thomas told him.

William shrugged. 'Don't think Sam would have said yes,' he responded. 'Sam is a mighty particular cuss.'

From the sound of his father's voice Thomas got the feeling that the old man had known about Herrick's feelings for Helen. But it was too late to make an issue out of it, especially since he and Helen had 'known' each other, as the sexual act was described in the Bible. Thomas knew what he owed her and he wasn't going to welsh on his debt, even if he didn't love her.

'You've never asked me why we took the herd to Christi,' William said, looking at him.

Thomas couldn't help smiling. 'And if I had, would you have answered?' he asked.

'Not likely,' his father responded, also smiling. 'Some things I taught you you've learned right well.'

'Some.'

William nodded. Then he said, 'There's a buyer in Christi who will pay twenty dollars a head for prime steers. That's twice as much as they'd bring in San Antone or Austin.'

'I didn't figure we were taking the herd to Christi just for a change of pace,' Thomas replied, preventing any of the admiration he felt for his father to seep into his voice. The old man was not only a damn good rancher, but he was also a shrewd businessman. No wonder the other ranchers around Paso Diablo went along with whatever he suggested.

'That's why,' William said, 'I was so worried about Johnson. If he had gotten his herd to Christi first the price would have dropped.'

'Then you figured on starting the drive early even before the trouble with Rusty?'

The old man nodded. 'But just a couple of days,' he said. 'Then when Rusty was killed and you —' He stopped. 'It was best that we started when we did.'

Thomas agreed.

'There's something else,' William told him.

'Oh?'

'Your brother Clem is probably there waiting for us,' he informed him.

'Really?' Thomas questioned. 'But why didn't you tell me before?'

'Wouldn't have made much difference,' the old man answered. 'We had to get there first. He came down by ship to New Orleans and then by stage to Christi, at least that was the way he said he'd be coming. He'll be staying at the Silver Spur Hotel.'

Thomas slapped his thigh. 'I'll sure be glad to see him! Seems like he's been away forever. It will be good riding back with him.'

'That's if he still remembers how to ride,' William laughed.

'He never did like riding much,' Thomas said, adding his laughter to that of the old man's. 'I remember the time he was thrown from a mustang he was trying to break. He wouldn't get back on him —' He stopped and asked, 'Did you write to John?'

William looked away and said, 'He's gone his way.'

The all-too-familiar hardness was back in his father's voice. Thomas stood up. He had asked the wrong question. 'All the same,' he said, sullenly, 'it will be good to see Clem.'

'Better take care of your mount,' William told him, looking out toward where the herd was bedded down for the night.

Thomas nodded, but the old man didn't look at him again, and he went back to his horse without saying anything else.

EIGHT

At nine o'clock the following morning Thomas rode up the busy main street of Corpus Christi to the Silver Spur Hotel. A few minutes later he was standing at the desk waiting for the room clerk to finish adding up the bill for a departing guest.

The Silver Spur was the newest hotel in the city and its lobby was huge, with potted plants in the corners, several sitting chairs, glittering crystal chandeliers hanging down from the ceiling on huge chains, and the walls covered with silver-colored paper. Even from where Thomas stood he could see the large bar at one end, and when he glanced at the other end he saw the dining room.

Thomas shook his head. He had never seen a place quite like it. Then he realized several of the people in the lobby were staring at him, especially the women, whose expressions of disdain were obvious. He turned his back toward them and impatiently waited for the clerk.

As soon as the guest had left Thomas said, 'Excuse me, I wonder if you could tell me in what room Mister Clem Carey is staying?'

The clerk, a small man in a black frock coat, looked at him. 'Is he expecting you?' he asked, sniffing at the air.

'That's twenty-two days on the trail,' Thomas told him. 'Now if you'd tell me where his room is, I'd be much obliged.'

'We don't permit our guests to be disturbed,' he said.

Thomas nodded. He didn't like the man's attitude, especially the way he sniffed at the air. But he kept his temper in check and said, 'I'm his brother. I think you have reservations for me and my father, William Carey.'

'If you'll sign the register,' the clerk said with a sudden toothy smile, 'I'll have one of the boys show you to your room.'

Thomas sighed. 'Now, my brother's room number, please?'

'He occupies three-thirty-two,' the big man said. 'That's right across the hall from yours.'

'And my father's?'

'Next to yours,' the clerk told him as he handed him the key to his room.

'He'll be along directly,' Thomas said. 'If I were you I wouldn't make the same mistake with him that you made with me. He's meaner than me, looks worse, and smells about the same.'

The clerk quickly assured him that his father would have no difficulty, and then asked if he had any baggage.

'Just what's on my horse,' he answered, 'and I'll get that later.'

Thomas left the desk and walked across the lobby with deliberate slowness to the steps near the bar-room. But when he reached the first landing and was sure he was out of sight, he quickened his pace until he was running up the remaining flights to the third floor.

The moment he found his brother's room Thomas began to pound on the door. 'Hey, Clem!' he shouted, 'it's Thomas … c'mon man, wake up! Hey, Clem?'

Clem was too intoxicated with the naked body of the woman in bed with him to pay the slightest bit of attention to the loud banging on the door and the louder bellowing of his name. What seemed like just a few moments ago, he and the woman were sleeping as soundly and innocently as children. But then she moved and her soft naked buttocks brushed against his manhood. The touch of that delicious softness was enough to waken him, and once awake he set about to satiate his desire. No man who called himself a man would do less!

He had just put his lips to the puckered nipple that budded out of the café-au-lait breast when the silence of the room and the intimacy of the moment were shattered by the boisterous clamor on the other side of the door.

The noise had destroyed the mood. Clem sensed the subtle change in the tone of the woman's body. What had been soft and yielding had, because of the clamor, become tense. He lifted his face from the naked breast and, looking back at the door with an angry glare, shouted, 'Damn it! Go away. I'm busy.'

'Not on your life,' came the answer. 'Clem, if you don't open the damn door I'll break it open.'

Clem recognized his brother's voice and leaped up. 'Thomas?' he called out.

Laughter followed his question, and then followed the reply, 'You'll find out as soon as you open the door.'

'Who is it?' the woman whispered, pulling the sheet over her nakedness.

'My brother,' he answered, leaving the bed. He slipped on a dressing gown. A few moments later the door was open.

'My God, you look a sight!' Clem exclaimed the moment he saw his brother.

'And smell worse!' Thomas added, taking hold of Clem's hand and shaking it violently.

'How's Pa?'

'Fine, just fine! And as ornery as ever.'

'He never changes.' Clem laughed. 'If he did I think he'd be sick. Where is he?'

'Selling off the herd we brought in,' Thomas said. 'He'll be along directly.'

'Then I best get moving,' Clem said, stepping back into the room.

'This is some fancy hotel,' he laughed, following Clem. 'Down in the lobby —' Then he saw the woman. She was a woman of color, and her dark eyes were focused on him.

'That's Dawn,' Clem explained. Then looking at the woman he said, 'Dawn, say hello to my brother Thomas.'

Dawn glanced at Clem.

'Don't be afraid of him,' he laughed. 'He's not half as bad as he looks and smells.'

'Hello, Mr Thomas,' she finally said.

Thomas nodded and touched the tip of his sombrero. 'Hello, Dawn,' he answered. Then he looked questioningly at his brother.

'I bought her in New Orleans,' he said. 'I was in the St Charles Hotel and she was on the auction block. I figured that I could get more here than what I paid for her in New Orleans. Just last night one of the men in the bar offered me fourteen hundred dollars. That would have been three hundred dollars more than I had paid. But the man wanted her for his house and I didn't want to do that to her.'

Thomas remained silent, but he felt the skin on his back begin to crawl. The idea of buying or selling a woman, or for that matter any human being, was completely against his nature. He glanced at Dawn and saw that she was completely impassive to his brother's comments.

Clem put his hand on Thomas' shoulder. 'Don't fret about her,' he said gently. 'I'll make sure her next master is a good man.'

'Pa isn't going to like it,' Thomas said, feeling the great distance between his brother and himself.

'That's why,' Clem said, 'I've got to take care of the whole business before he shows up.'

'You had better,' Thomas warned.

Clem smiled. 'So the old man still has a temper, eh?' Clem asked.

Thomas nodded.

Clem shook his head. 'For the life of me,' he said, 'I'll never understand his attitude. He dearly loves this country, but his feelings about slavery are —'

'You going to sell me this morning?' Dawn asked.

Clem turned toward her. 'My pa,' he laughed, 'would throw nine kinds of a fit if he saw you.'

'Don't he own any slaves?' she asked.

'No,' Thomas answered. 'He doesn't own any slaves.'

She looked questioningly at Clem.

He shrugged and said, 'He has strange views for a southerner.' Then he asked Thomas if he had eaten breakfast yet.

'At sunup,' Thomas answered.

Clem laughed. 'Thank God I didn't have to go on any cattle drive!' he said. 'I don't know how you stand it.' He shook his head. 'But each man to his own choice, right?'

'Then why not give her a choice?' he said, pointing down at Dawn. The words were out of his mouth before he could stop them.

'You *are* your father's son!' Clem exclaimed good-naturedly. And then, putting his arm around Thomas, he said, 'This is the South, and if a gentleman has need of a companion for his pleasure and the price to pay for it then he's entitled to it. Now would you have me set Dawn on her own resources?' He slipped his arm off his brother's shoulders 'She has only one skill, one resource that's of any value, and that's to please a man in or out of bed. Why, just looking at her is a pleasurable experience. Dawn,' he said, stepping close to the bed, 'show my brother Thomas what he wants to deny other men from enjoying.'

'That won't be necessary,' Thomas told him.

'Show him, Dawn,' Clem insisted, ignoring his brother.

Dawn threw back the sheet and lay there naked.

Thomas couldn't help but react. Her body was exquisitely formed, and even the dark triangular patch of hair at the base of her torso was lovely to look at. She reminded him of Lisa, and his lips and throat were suddenly dry.

'Even you,' Clem smiled, noting the effect of Dawn's nakedness on his brother, 'can't deny either her beauty or the legitimacy of my views.'

Thomas shook his head. 'She's yours,' he admitted. 'But I still hold with Pa —'

'Sooner or later,' Clem said, walking over to the bed and placing his hand gently on Dawn's naked breast, 'you're going to have to make a choice…' The tone of his voice had become harder. 'The North won't be satisfied until every slave is free.' With his hand still on the woman's breast, he faced his brother. 'And the South won't let that happen, at least not without a fight. Mark my words, Thomas, there will be a war over it, and then you will have to choose. I have already made my choice,' he said, turning back to look at the nude woman.

For a few moments neither of them spoke.

Thomas didn't know what to say. He was no match for Clem when it came to discussing the issue of slavery — or, for that matter, any other issue. He felt sorry for the woman, but he wasn't about to argue over her with his brother. Finally he said that he wanted to go to his room to bathe and shave.

'Fine!' Clem exclaimed. 'That will give me and Dawn time to dress. Then the three of us can go down and find a buyer for Dawn. With you along, I'm sure to find the right kind of a man for her.'

'I'll be ready in about an hour,' Thomas told him.

'Excellent!' Clem exclaimed, and he escorted Thomas to the door. 'By the way,' he laughed, 'I forgot to congratulate you on your forthcoming marriage to the Wicker girl. As I remember her, she was a pretty little thing.'

'Thanks,' Thomas responded flatly.

Clem cocked his head to one side. 'You don't seem terribly excited about it,' he said.

'Seems like the thing most men do sooner or later,' Thomas answered with a shrug.

Clem balled his fist and playfully drove it into his brother's shoulder. 'I never had you pegged for an early marriage,' he said. 'Come to think about it, I seem to recall that you were cattin' around with that saloon girl … what's her name?'

'Lisa.'

'Yes,' Clem said, 'that's the one.' Then suddenly he glanced back at Dawn. 'She kind of looks like her, don't she?'

'Not much,' Thomas lied. 'Not much at all.'

'Well,' Clem said, 'we'll have a lot to talk about once I transact my business.'

Thomas smiled and stepped out into the hallway. 'I'll see you in about an hour,' he said.

Clem nodded and closed the door.

A moment later Thomas heard the key turn in the latch. He knew with absolute certainty that Clem had gone back into bed with Dawn.

With a deep sigh he crossed the hallway and let himself into the room. What Clem had said about making a choice if it came to a showdown between the North and the South bothered him, teasing his brain the way a fly torments a horse, and like that animal, Thomas couldn't rid himself of it.

There was no dearth of men eager to pay a good price for Dawn, and she was quickly sold to a middle-aged gentleman. Thomas was surprised at the ease with which Clem consummated the transaction and with how easily Dawn accepted the fact that she belonged to another man.

As soon as Clem received his payment he and Thomas strolled through the busy streets of Christi. Thomas thoroughly enjoyed being with his brother. In the two short years that Clem had been up north studying law he had developed into a man of the world. Even though he still spoke with a Texas drawl, his manner of speaking was obviously that of a well-educated man. Several times people turned to gape at them, and Thomas realized that they must seem peculiar, since he was rigged out like a vaquero and Clem was dressed in eastern clothes, a dark, wide-brimmed planter's hat and Texas riding boots. His brother looked more like a gentleman than anyone he had ever seen, and he didn't even bother to wear a gun.

When Thomas asked him why he wasn't wearing one, Clem answered that he didn't look for trouble and trouble didn't look for him.

'I wish I could say the same,' Thomas commented with a chuckle, and then he told him about the various gunfights in which he had become involved.

'Seems to me,' Clem said, 'that you had good cause.'

'Pa thinks I'm always on the prod,' Thomas explained.

'He rides you real hard, doesn't he?'

Thomas shrugged. 'It's his way, I guess.'

Clem made no comment, but then he asked, 'How come you decided to get married?'

'I didn't,' Thomas answered, and then he explained the situation to his brother. 'It finally came down to the choice he gave me. Either I marry Helen or I leave the ranch.' He took a deep breath and said, 'But now I don't even have that choice.'

Clem stopped and looked at him questioningly.

'I guess you know what I mean,' Thomas said, looking down at the dusty brown earth.

'You mean you and Helen —'

Feeling like a small boy who had been caught with his hand in the cookie jar, he nodded and said, 'I promised her that we'd be married the week after I got back.' He looked up at his brother. 'It was the proper thing to do, wasn't it?'

'In your circumstances,' Clem replied, with a nod, 'it was the *only* thing you could do.' And then he started to walk again.

'Have you heard from John?' Thomas asked as they turned back toward the hotel.

'I was wondering when you'd get around to asking about him,' Clem said.

Thomas laughed. 'To tell the truth,' he commented, 'I was hoping you'd tell me before I asked.'

'John, I'm afraid, has truly left the fold,' Clem said.

'I don't understand.'

'You know he's a journalist?'

'Pa told me that,' Thomas said, 'after you wrote to him about it.'

'I saw John just before I wrote that letter,' Clem told him. 'He was on his way to England.'

'Is that a fact?'

'He went there on an assignment for the newspaper.'

'Isn't that something!'

'His newspaper is strongly abolitionist,' Clem said, 'and so is John. To hear him talk you'd think he was born and bred in the North. I tell you, Thomas, I couldn't believe he was my brother.' Clem shook his head. 'He wrote to me several times, but I didn't see the point of answering his letters. We were never really very close, even though we're brothers.' Then he glanced at Thomas. 'You liked him, didn't you?'

'I still do,' Thomas replied, looking straight at his brother.

Clem smiled. 'And so you should,' he said, 'but remember what I said about making your choice. The time for that is coming faster than you think.'

Thomas shrugged. 'Then I guess I'll wait for it to come,' he told Clem. And then, more to change the subject than anything else, he said, 'Pa must be back at the hotel right now. I think we should go over there and see.'

'A good idea!' Clem exclaimed, and he quickened his stride. But just before they entered the lobby he stopped and wheeled around.

'What's wrong?' Thomas questioned.

'I have the damndest feeling that we're being followed,' he said.

No sooner had his brother spoken than Thomas faced the street. His gun was out and ready, but no one seemed interested in him or Clem.

'Good God!' Clem exclaimed in a nervous whisper. 'Put that thing away.'

Thomas didn't move a muscle. His eyes flicked over every face in view.

'It was just a feeling,' Clem said.

Thomas caught sight of a tall man in a black sombrero. He was standing some distance up the street, with his back turned toward the hotel. There was something vaguely familiar about him.

'Put the gun away,' Clem told him again.

Thomas nodded and slid the heavy Navy Colt back into its holster.

'You don't hesitate much, do you?' Clem said, slapping his younger brother on the back.

Thomas shook his head, and then he asked, 'Is anyone after you?'

'Hell, no!' Clem laughed. 'I'm a peace-loving man. Come on, let's go up and see if Pa is here.'

William was genuinely glad to see Clem, and after several moments of hearty handshaking and back-slapping he suggested they all go down to the bar for a drink.

'Amen to that!' Clem said. 'I am as dry as an old well in the middle of August.'

They sat down at a table in the corner and William ordered a bottle of the best whiskey the hotel sold. As soon as the glasses were filled he toasted the forthcoming marriage. 'May it be happy and fruitful,' he said, looking hard at his youngest son.

Thomas nodded and reluctantly lifted the glass.

Then William toasted to the successful finish of the drive, and wound up by saying, 'And may there be lots more like it.'

They all drank to that, and finally Clem toasted to the good luck and happiness of the Carey family, and the three of them drank to that.

The afternoon passed swiftly, and when they had drunk more than three-quarters of the bottle William reminded Thomas that he wanted to bring something back to Helen.

Thomas shook his head. 'I don't know what to buy,' he said.

'Anything you bring,' the old man said, 'will make her happy.' He cast his eyes on Clem. 'You go with him,' he told him. 'I'm sure you'll know what to buy a woman.'

'I don't need no help,' Thomas said, getting to his feet.

'Sure you do,' Clem said in a conciliatory tone. 'Pa is just trying to tell us to scaddle for a while.' And he winked broadly.

The whiskey had boggled Thomas' ability to think straight, but he did catch the drift of what his brother said. Strange, he could never imagine his father in bed with a woman, doing the things that he and Lisa had done. Lisa! Her name caused his gut to ball up into a tight knot.

Bleary-eyed, he looked at his father. 'Have a good time, old man,' he said. 'Have a good time.'

'Leave Pa be,' Clem said, taking his brother by the arm. 'You don't want to rile him none.'

Thomas shook his head and let Clem lead him from the table. But as soon as they were out of the bar he pulled free of Clem and told him that he could stand.

The fresh air cleared his head some, and with Clem's aid he bought a beautiful silk shawl for Helen. He would have bought another for Lisa if Clem had not been there to stop him. But on the way back to the hotel Thomas said, 'That shawl was made for a woman like Lisa and not one like Helen.'

'C'mon boy,' Clem said, 'let's get back to the hotel. You'll feel better after a couple of hours' sleep.'

'Sure,' Thomas agreed. 'I'm never much good unless I have my afternoon nap.'

Clem laughed. 'Since when do you take afternoon naps?' Clem asked.

'Oh, but I have!' Thomas exclaimed, and put his finger to his lips. 'Mustn't tell Pa,' he whispered. 'But the times I spent in the afternoon with Lisa were the best ... know what I mean?'

'Yes,' Clem said, 'I do know what you mean.'

Thomas was quiet for a moment and then he said, 'She was mine then.'

Clem managed to get his brother upstairs, into his room, and finally into bed.

'Thanks,' Thomas said, looking up at his brother with a smile on his face. 'Thanks, Clem.' He closed his eyes. 'I wish John were here, too. Then we'd really be a family again.'

'I'll write and tell him what you said.'

Thomas nodded and, turning on his side, fell asleep.

Clem stood over his younger brother for some time and wondered if he should have a talk with his father about him. He decided not to interfere. It would be different if he had intended to remain at the ranch, but he was going back to Boston at the end of the summer. His way of life was already considerably different from that of Thomas and his father. Besides, he didn't want to spoil his stay by incurring William's anger. He remembered just how mean and stubborn his father could be.

No, this wasn't his problem, and he decided to leave it alone. But nonetheless he couldn't help feeling sorry for Thomas. God knows it was a helluva way for the boy to enter the blessed state of matrimony.

Thomas slept well until a dream interrupted. And then, with vivid clarity, he saw the tall man in the black sombrero again. He watched him slowly turn, and then he saw his face. He recognized him. He knew who it was.

He bolted upright, but in the very next instant the memory of the dream was gone, and with it the name of the man. All he was left with was the uncomfortable feeling of having forgotten something he should have remembered.

He looked around him. From the way the room was steeped in dark gray, Thomas realized he had been asleep several hours. He went to the wash basin and freshened up. Then he left the room, crossed the hall to Clem's room, and knocked at the door. No one answered. He tried his father's room, and no one was there either. He shrugged and went downstairs, where he found both of them in the bar seated at the same table that the three of them had occupied earlier.

'Well,' Thomas announced, 'I'm bright-eyed and bushy-tailed now, so why don't we go and eat?'

Clem was on his feet before anyone else could speak. 'I'm already there,' he laughed.

The three of them walked across the lobby and into the restaurant.

When the waiter came, each of them ordered a double steak and potatoes and Thomas asked for black coffee. Thomas realized that Clem had an easy way with the old man, making him talk on everything from the ranch to asking what Boston was like. By the time the steaks came William had finally questioned Clem about John.

Clem answered his father pretty much as he had answered Thomas, including what he had said about having to make a choice.

William chewed on his steak without interrupting his son. Though he was pleased that John wrote things other people read, the bad feelings between them ran too deep for either one to forgive the other. But he had to admit that if he agreed with John about anything it would be on the issue of slavery.

He looked at Clem and said, 'If you write to your brother, tell him I asked about him, and that I wish him good health and good luck.'

'I'll do that.'

'I'm a Texan,' William commented, 'and Texas is part of the South; that, I guess, makes me a southerner too. But that doesn't necessarily mean I have to like or do everything other southerners do or like, does it?'

'Naturally not,' Clem answered. 'But the South stands on the issue of slavery. Surely you see that?'

'Maybe yes and maybe no,' William said, cocking his head slightly to one side. 'Now you take my friend Sam Wicker; he owns slaves but he treats them right well. I can't stop him from owning them.'

'That's exactly the point,' Clem responded. 'The North wants to put an end to slavery in the South, and they haven't got the right.'

William's lips pulled apart into a tight smile. 'Then I guess I didn't have the right to do what I did on the way to the hotel this morning.'

'What was that, Pa?' Thomas asked. He knew his father well enough to know that it was something unusual.

'I was with Cowper,' he said. 'The two of us were walking away from the cattle pens and had just turned into the main street when we saw this middle-aged gentleman with a young woman of color. She was a pretty thing, with skin the color of light coffee and long black hair. She was lagging behind him and he kept urging her to walk faster, but his stride was twice the size of hers. Anyway, he became angry and began beating her with his cane.'

'The bastard!' Thomas exclaimed, and he looked at Clem, whose face had become tightly drawn.

'I didn't like what he was doing,' William continued, 'so I went up to him and —'

'You tried to stop him?' Thomas asked.

William nodded. 'But that just made him angrier,' he said. 'He told me he had just bought her and she had to learn his ways.'

'Then what happened?' Clem questioned, hardly moving his lips as he spoke.

'Well,' the old man admitted, 'I guess I shouldn't have done what I did, but I was angry too.'

Thomas hung on his father's words. He was impatient to hear what had happened next.

'It ain't fitting for a man to beat a woman,' William said. 'I told that man that, but he wouldn't listen. He said she was his property and he could do with her whatever he wanted.' He shook his head, almost as though he were attempting to deny the entire episode. 'Well, I grabbed hold of his cane and broke it across my leg. Then Cowper and me went our way up the street.'

Thomas rapped the table with the palm of his hand. 'By God, I would have done a helluva lot more to the son-of-a-bitch.' The sound of his hand striking the table and the loudness of his voice immediately attracted attention to the table, but he didn't care. From the way William glared at those who looked at them, Thomas knew that his father felt the same way.

'The law was on the man's side,' Clem said, softly but firmly.

'Then the law is wrong,' Thomas shot at him.

'Please,' Clem said to his younger brother, 'lower your voice. There's no need to have everyone in the place partner to our conversation.'

'All right,' Thomas responded. 'I'll keep my voice down.'

'What would you have done?' William asked.

'Killed the old bastard,' Thomas answered hotly.

William eyed him coldly. 'And probably would have been killed in turn,' he said. Then he shifted his gaze to Clem and waited for a reply.

'Try to reason with the man,' Clem finally said.

'Bah!' Thomas exclaimed in disgust.

'Give your brother a chance to speak,' William told his youngest son.

'He would have listened to reason,' Clem maintained. 'After all, she won't be much good to him if she's all bruised.'

William shook his head. 'I'm afraid his kind has only one use in mind for her,' he said. 'And when he finishes with her I don't think she'll be much good for anything. Tell me, Clem, what would you do if he didn't listen to reason?'

'Let well enough alone,' Clem answered, 'and go my way. I'm not a violent man, and I believe in obeying the law even if I don't agree with the way it is being administered.'

William didn't answer. He picked up the fork and popped the piece of steak into his mouth, but it had turned cold and lost its taste. He chewed it slowly and tried to think of something else to talk about, but couldn't. He looked at his sons. Clem continued to eat, but not with the same gusto that he had earlier, while Thomas stared down at the plate, his jaw set and his face hard with anger.

NINE

None of the Careys had much to say for the remainder of the time they were at the table. As soon as William finished his coffee he went up to his room, telling his sons that he was tired.

'I thought you said,' Thomas told Clem when their father was out of the dining room, 'that he would be kind to Dawn.'

'He looked like a gentleman,' Clem answered, pouring more coffee into his cup.

Thomas snorted.

'All right,' Clem admitted, 'I made a mistake and I am truly sorry.'

'Don't tell me,' Thomas replied. 'Tell Dawn. She's the one who was caned, to say nothing of the fact that she was the one who shared your bed —'

'I'd rather not continue this conversation,' Clem told him. 'But believe me, I never mistreated her — or, for that matter, any Negro. That's not my way.' Then he lowered his eyes. 'Besides,' he said, 'I've come all this way from Boston to be with you and Pa, not to argue whether slavery is just or unjust.'

Thomas nodded and apologized for jumping on Clem.

'Even in the same family,' Clem said with a smile, 'there are differences of opinion. Now what do you say to going out and having a good time?'

'I'd like that,' Thomas answered.

'There's a place not far from here called the Brasadero. I was told that the women are the best in Christi, the gambling is run straight and the whiskey is high-grade.'

'Sounds too good to be true.'

'Let's find out for ourselves,' Clem said, gesturing to the waiter. When the man came to the table, he asked for the bill and signed his name and room number on it. 'I guess we can go now,' he told Thomas.

The two of them left the restaurant, walked through the lobby and out into the cool night air.

'My God,' Thomas exclaimed. 'Will you look at all the people!'

Pedestrians of every sort crowded the wooden walkways, and the streets were still busy with the flow of wagons and horses. Some of the wagons carried blazing torches, others made do with small lamps that glowed yellow in the sultry night air. But for the most part the walkways were illuminated by the light coming through the windows of the various stores, though at each intersection were lamps supplied by the city that were suspended out over the street.

'This isn't Paso Diablo,' Clem reminded him. 'Christi is a city and cities don't have time to sleep.'

Thomas was too busy looking at all of the people to answer, and then he felt Clem tug at his sleeve. He started to face his brother.

'Don't look at me,' Clem told him, and then he added, 'I'm sure we're being followed.'

Thomas kept his head turned to the street. 'Did you get a look at him?' he asked.

'Just for a moment,' Clem said, 'when I glanced back over my shoulder. He's a tall man —'

'With a black sombrero?' Thomas asked, remembering the man in his dream and the one he had seen earlier.

'Yes,' Clem responded. 'But how did you know?'

'Just keep walking,' he told his brother.

'Do you know him?'

'No. But I saw a tall man with the same color sombrero just before we went into the hotel,' he said. 'He had his back to me, so I couldn't see his face, but nonetheless he looked familiar.'

'But why would anyone want to follow us?' Clem questioned.

'Maybe it was someone who saw you sell Dawn and figured you might be carrying a fat bankroll?'

'I didn't see anyone watching us.'

Thomas shrugged. 'Sometimes we don't see those who watch,' he said. 'Anyway, if he's following us and we know he is, then we hold a few cards he hadn't counted on.' And then he asked how far they had to go until they reached the Brasadero.

'It's still some distance from here,' Clem answered. 'You don't think he'll try something out here on the main street?'

'*He* won't,' Thomas answered, 'but *we* will. There's a side street up ahead,' he said. 'When we reach it we'll swing into it. Stay in the shadows as much as you can. Understand?'

'Yes. But why —'

'Just do what I said,' Thomas answered impatiently. 'And for God's sake stay close against the building. He comes after us — well, we'll see if he does.'

When they reached the intersection, the two of them turned up the darkened side street. Thomas gestured Clem toward the side of the building, where it was dark, while he himself stood a short distance in from the main street.

'Is he coming?' Clem called softly.

Thomas didn't answer. His heart was banging away in his chest, and his throat was very dry. He held his hand poised above the butt of his gun. A few moments passed and no one came. He waited a while longer. Whoever was following them should have come, or at least passed across the intersection —

unless, of course, he had no intention of having a showdown then and there.

'It's all right,' he called out to Clem.

'You didn't see him?' his brother asked as he came up to him.

'No,' Thomas answered and ventured to suggest that maybe Clem had imagined someone was following them.

'Maybe,' Clem replied. But Thomas knew that his brother didn't believe it, and neither did he. Clem was too level-headed to be spooked by the same thing twice in one day.

By the time they reached the Brasadero the two of them needed a drink and they went straight to the bar, where there were several other drovers who had been on the drive with Thomas. They greeted him warmly and some of them remembered Clem.

Several rounds of drinks were brought before Clem spotted a young blonde-haired woman looking at him. He poked Thomas in the ribs and nodded in the direction of the woman. 'See what I mean when I told you they had the best of everything here?'

'Not my type,' Thomas said. 'But if you're interested I'll wait for you at the table and try my luck.'

Clem nodded. 'Don't become impatient,' he said. 'I don't like to rush things.'

'I'll be around when you're finished.'

'If you see anything you like,' Clem told him with a smile, 'help yourself. I promise not to tell Helen.'

'Wouldn't bother me none if you did,' Thomas replied. 'But if you stand here much longer talking to me you're going to be caught short. I see one of those men from the ships looking at her.'

Clem laughed and started across the room toward the young woman. Then suddenly he saw the tall man in the black sombrero. He stopped, but the man had already moved out of the shadows close to the wall.

Thomas had watched his brother for a moment and then turned back to his companions at the bar. Suddenly he sensed something had changed. Prickles raced down his back, and he looked up at the mirror and behind the bar. He saw that Clem had stopped, and then Thomas heard his name called. The men on either side of him moved away.

'Turn around,' the man ordered.

Thomas remained frozen at the bar.

'Turn around, you whelp!'

The voice had a familiar ring to it. He tried to see who it was in the mirror, but the man was still in too much shadow.

'Who are you?' Thomas asked, still keeping his back toward the man.

'I thought by now you'd have knowed,' the man answered.

The voice sounded familiar, but not so familiar that Thomas could identify it.

'Turn around, or are you yellow like I said you were?'

'Herrick?'

'You're slow, boy, real slow.'

'I thought you went back to Mr Wicker,' Thomas said, stalling for time.

Herrick laughed. 'Do you think he'd have me after you and your pa sent me packin'? No, I came here instead. I've been waiting for you, Thomas — all this time I've been waiting. Now turn around.'

Thomas raised his hands and slowly faced the man. As soon as he had completed the turn he saw him. 'Now what?' he asked.

'I'm going to teach you a lesson you'll never forget,' Herrick said. 'Don't worry none, I don't aim to kill you. I just want to bust you up so that you'll remember me for the rest of your life.' Suddenly the whistling sound of a bull whip trembled in the air of the silent room and was immediately followed by a snap-like explosion. 'I'm goin' to whip the hide off of you, boy.'

'You have no cause,' Thomas said.

'You give me cause enough,' Herrick said. 'First you take my woman and then you have your old man give me the sack.'

The fact that Herrick was still standing in the shadow and that he was too far away to use the whip registered in Thomas' brain with absolute clarity. But in the next instant Herrick moved, and the whip made a humming sound as it cut through the air and slashed across Thomas' midsection, cutting through his clothes and drawing blood. He dropped his hands and doubled over to protect himself. The next two lashes tore across his back and cut through his skin with the searing pain. He cried aloud and fell to the floor.

The whip came down and snaked across his shoulders. Herrick came nearer and worked his arm like a piston. Each time the lash found its mark. 'That's where you belong,' Herrick shouted. 'On the floor, crawling around like an animal.' He swung the whip again.

Thomas screamed.

'Listen to the little bastard yell,' Herrick shouted to the onlookers. 'Just listen to him —' He stopped. Thomas had grabbed hold of the whip. Herrick tried to jerk it free. Horrified, he saw Thomas struggle to his feet.

Then suddenly Herrick dropped the whip and went for his gun. But Thomas saw him. He was on his feet now.

'Draw,' he said in an ice-hard voice, 'and you're a dead man.'

Herrick stood still.

'Pick up the whip, Clem,' Thomas said.

Clem hesitated.

'Pick it up and give it to me,' Thomas told him. When he had it in his hand he said, 'I took ten from you, Herrick. Now you'll take twenty from me.'

'No!' Herrick shouted. He turned and started to run. Thomas rushed after him and with the first lash caught him by his legs and brought him down. He delivered lash after lash and each one brought a shout of pain from the prostrate man.

'For the love of God,' Clem shouted, 'let him be.'

'Sure,' Thomas answered, 'when I'm done with him.'

Herrick passed out before Thomas finished, but that didn't stop him. Finally he laid the last stroke on and threw the whip to the floor. Dripping with sweat and wet with his own blood, Thomas turned to the bar and finished off his drink. Then he staggered past Herrick, looked at the bloody mess he had made of the man's face, and rushed out into the street to vomit.

TEN

Thomas married Helen on the last Sunday in June. The ceremony took place directly after the morning services, and the pastor made a long speech about the holy state of matrimony before he got around to saying the actual words that tied them together for life.

Even though it was late morning the small church was sweltering and filled with a variety of human smells. Clem had prevailed upon Thomas that morning to use cologne, and he was sure that everyone in the congregation smelled him.

For the occasion he was rigged out in new clothes, but because he wasn't wearing his chaps and gun Thomas felt oddly naked. Now and then he glanced at Helen standing at his side. She was dressed in white and looked incredibly cool, though her face did seem whiter than usual.

Several times during the ceremony Thomas' thoughts drifted away from what was happening and he found himself thinking about Lisa. Since the day he had left her shanty he had not gone back to see her, though more than once he had started to. But somewhere between the ranch and Paso Diablo he had always changed his mind, even when he had intended to give her the lace shawl that he had bought for Helen. The shawl was still in its original box in the back of his drawer. Somehow he couldn't bring himself to give it to Helen. It seemed to him the shawl rightfully belonged to Lisa.

'Thomas Carey?' the pastor called.

The sound of his name wrenched him out of his thoughts. He blinked and gave the man his attention. The marriage ceremony had begun.

More words from the pastor, and then finally he asked, 'Do you, Thomas Carey, take this woman, Helen Wicker, to be your lawful wedded wife, to love, honor and cherish in sickness and in health until death do you part?'

Thomas hesitated. His mind seemed to have gotten stuck on the words *lawful wedded wife*. Several moments passed. He sensed the growing uneasiness of the people behind him. He glanced at Helen. She was looking up at him, her lips parted with a kind of breathless anxiety.

He nodded, looked at the pastor and said, 'I do.' A sigh of relief trembled through the congregation.

'And do you, Helen Wicker,' the pastor said, looking at her, 'take this man, Thomas Carey, in sickness and in health, to love, honor, and obey until death do you part?'

'I do,' she answered quickly.

Then Clem, the best man, came forward and handed Thomas the simple gold ring that had belonged to their mother. More words, and then Thomas slipped the ring on Helen's finger.

'I now pronounce you man and wife,' the pastor said. 'What God hath joined together let no man put asunder.'

Helen stood facing Thomas, waiting for him to lift the veil from her face and kiss her. She saw the agonized look of confusion on his face. Was he just shy or was it something more — something that she was not prepared to meet on her wedding day? Rather than remain there in front of the entire congregation she took matters into her own hands and whispered, 'Kiss me!'

'Yes,' Clem joined in, 'everyone is waiting —'

Thomas lifted the veil from Helen's face and put his lips to hers momentarily. A loud cheer went up from the spectators. Helen placed her arms around Thomas' neck, hoping that he would hold her closer. He did, and she silently thanked God.

'That's enough, brother,' Clem said, tapping Thomas on the shoulder. 'Time to let the best man kiss the bride.'

Thomas released her, and Clem kissed her. Then her father and his father kissed Helen. When that was over they shook his hand and pounded him on the back, wishing him the best of luck.

After a few minutes they walked down the aisle and out into the hot, dazzling sun. People showered them with rice and strips of paper as they made their way to the buggy. The wedding reception was going to be at the Wicker place, and everyone was invited. Sam even had hired four musicians who came all the way from Austin just to make sure that there would be enough music.

Thomas helped Helen up into the buggy and took the seat beside her. He flicked the reins over the horse's back and the animal started off at a high-stepping trot down the length of the main street.

A few moments after they left the church they passed the Broken Horn Saloon. Tiny was standing out front. Thomas waved, and the barkeep gestured with his thumb toward the upper story.

Thomas raised his eyes. Lisa was in a window looking down at him and Helen. He tried to drop his eyes, but couldn't.

'That's her, isn't it?' Helen questioned in a slight voice, looking up at the woman who had been her husband's whore.

'Who?' Thomas asked, looking at Helen.

'The woman — I mean Lisa.'

'I didn't see her,' he said, hoping she would not challenge his lie.

'She's very beautiful,' Helen said.

He lifted the whip and was about to bring it down hard on the horse's back when Helen stayed his hand. 'It's not right to whip him for what you have done,' she told him.

Thomas set the whip back in its metal holder. Hunched forward, he drove in silence, feeling the heat of his anger deep inside of him.

When they came in sight of the Wicker place Helen linked her arm with his and, moving closer to him, said, 'I'm sorry. I should not have said anything back there in Paso Diablo.'

Thomas didn't move or say anything. He was angry with himself for having looked up at Lisa when he should have cast his eyes on Helen. He was angry with Lisa for having been there. What good had it been for her to see him with Helen? Didn't she realize that each time he thought about her his guts felt as though they were being roasted over a slow fire?

'Truly,' Helen said, 'I am sorry.'

'No need to be,' he answered sharply. 'We're married, aren't we?'

'Yes,' Helen said. 'We're married.' She took a deep breath and slowly exhaled. That she would have done something on the day of her marriage to make her husband angry would have been beyond her ability to imagine. She had to say something to him that would smother the anger in him and give him a glimpse of the happiness Helen felt sure she could give him. 'Rein up for a moment,' she said.

He looked questioningly at her.

'Just for a moment or two.'

He nodded and, pulling in on the reins, stopped the horse. 'All right,' he said. 'I —'

Helen looked up at him. 'I love you, Thomas,' she said, working hard to keep the catch in her voice under control lest it develop into a sob. 'As the pastor said, "for better or for worse in sickness and in health," I love you.' She took another deep breath and, after she exhaled, said, 'If I didn't, I would have never let you —' She stopped and cast her eyes down to her lap. 'I did it to make you happy…' Then she raised her eyes and looked into his. 'I told you once and I will tell you again,' she told him, 'there's enough love in me for the both of us. I hope and pray to God that you will someday come to love me as I love you. But until you do, all I ask is that you be kind to me.' In spite of her control her body trembled. 'Give me a chance and I promise you'll not regret it ever.'

'I know you will,' he said, feeling ashamed of himself for having made her unhappy. He slipped his arm free of hers and placed it around her shoulders. 'Don't take on so,' he told her softly. 'It's me, not you.' He kissed her forehead. 'Give me time to get used to being married. After all,' he chuckled, 'we've only been married about an hour.'

'I could have sworn it was longer,' she said with a smile. 'Maybe two hours.'

He nodded and gently slapped the horse's rump with the reins.

After the wedding reception at the Wicker place Thomas and Helen left for the Carey ranch, which they would have to themselves for the honeymoon period.

Helen waited for Thomas while he unhitched the horse and led it to the stable. The day was rapidly fading and the soft gray light of evening displaced the dazzling glare of the sun. Except for the sound of the wind, a great quietness hung over the earth. It was almost too quiet to be real. But Helen knew that she wasn't dreaming, that the low structure in front of her was to be her home from then until God called her. It was where she would bring her children into the world and watch them grow into good, strong men. She smiled at her thoughts. Why men only? Perhaps she could have a daughter? But first she would want to give Thomas a son.

She heaved a great sigh of contentment and realized that her life was just beginning. And with God's help it would be beautiful.

The door to the stable squeaked and she turned toward it. Thomas had pushed it shut and was now walking toward her.

'The place seems awfully strange with no one around,' he said.

'Maria is here, isn't she?'

'Probably in her house,' he said with a nod, and started for the door.

Helen followed alongside, and then to her surprise and delight he scooped her up and carried her across the threshold. As he started to set her down on her feet she clung to him.

'Thank you,' she whispered. 'Thank you.' And she kissed him. 'Now you can set me down.'

'I'll get your belongings from the buggy,' Thomas told her, and he went back out again. Just before he swung the heavy trunk on to his shoulder he paused. He felt skittish, as he had the very first time he lay with a woman. Maybe that was a good sign.

'Is everything all right?' Helen called from the doorway.

'Yes,' he answered, shouldering the trunk and returning to the house. 'I'll set them down in our room.'

Helen followed him. He placed the trunk against the wall and asked her if she wanted anything to eat or drink.

'Nothing,' she answered. Her heart suddenly began to race. She saw the way he was looking at her. She reached up and undid the ribbons that held her bonnet, and then she removed it.

'Would you like me to light a lamp?' he asked.

Helen shook her head. She didn't know what to say or do. His stare was so intense that she felt certain he could see through her clothing.

Thomas wanted to see her naked, not only because she was his wife but also because he hoped to experience with her the passion he had with Lisa. But he dared not tell her to undress in front of him; that would be treating her like a whore. A decent woman never exposed her naked body to her husband, at least not while the two of them were out of bed.

He took a deep breath and said, 'I think I'll see if Maria left any coffee.'

'All right,' she said, and watched him leave the room. A moment later the door closed and she was alone. Immediately she began to undress.

Thomas had no need of coffee or anything else. It was his way of giving her the time she needed to get out of the clothes she was wearing and slip on a nightgown. While he waited for Helen he removed his boots and everything else except his pants. Bare-chested, he walked back and forth across the length of the main room. From time to time he glanced at the closed door.

He realized that a short while ago when he was in the room with Helen he had actually wanted her, and now as he prowled up and down he could feel his desire for her become more intense. Perhaps now that he had a wife he would be able to put Lisa out of his mind and would not be haunted by the memory of their lovemaking.

He stopped pacing and remembered the old saying that still waters run deep. Helen was a quiet woman, that much he already knew. He hoped her passion would be equal to his, enough to make him forget what he had experienced with Lisa. If that happened then maybe he would come to love her.

Thomas clenched his fists and closed his eyes. If he had been a God-fearing man he would have prayed to the Almighty for His intervention. But Thomas did not believe in God. He put his faith and trust in his own strength and ability to do whatever had to be done.

The sound of the bedroom door opening made him open his eyes and fists. He turned toward it.

'Thomas?' Helen called, stepping into the main room.

'Yes,' he answered, stunned at the sight of her.

She started to move toward him.

'No,' he said. 'Just stay there. I want to look at you.'

She wore a full-length, long-sleeved white gown that was open at the neck just enough to reveal the valley between her girlish breasts. Her long blonde hair was loose and cascaded down to her shoulders.

'Is anything wrong?' she asked.

'No,' he replied, going to her. 'I just wanted to look at you.'

Taking her in his arms, he pressed her to his bare chest. His lips touched hers and he felt the soft push of her breasts against him.

Suddenly the front door burst open.

'Now ain't that a sight for sore eyes!' a man exclaimed.

Helen screamed.

Thomas shoved Helen back and started for the rifle above the fireplace.

'Easy there! There's more'n one gun on ya.'

The man at the door entered the house and two others followed him. 'Make some light,' he told one of his companions. 'Mighty nice place 'ere,' he said. 'Mighty nice.'

'What do you want, Zeb?' Thomas asked.

'Heard you were marryin', so naturally I came to pay my respects,' Zeb said. 'I kinda figure I owe you somethin'.'

'Who is he?' Helen asked, cowering close to the wall near the fireplace.

'Go a'ead an' tell 'er,' Zeb said.

'Just a ranch hand,' Thomas said.

Zeb laughed. 'You boys 'ear 'im?' He stepped in front of Thomas. 'You can't even tell 'er da truth.' He balled his fist and drove it into Thomas' stomach.

'Oh, God!' Helen screamed. She ran to Thomas, but Zeb grabbed her arm and flung her back against the wall.

Thomas gasped for breath. The blow had doubled him up, but he fought to keep on his feet.

'I'll tell you 'oo I am,' Zeb said. 'I'm the kin of the man 'e gunned down at da Broken 'Orn.'

'It was a fair fight,' Thomas said. 'You were there. You saw.'

'I didn't see nothin',' Zeb said, smashing his fist into Thomas' face.

Blood gushed from Thomas' nose. The room seemed to blur.

''E also kilt my friend,' Zeb said.

'What do you want?' Helen asked.

'Like I already said,' Zeb answered, 'I got somet'in' for 'im.' He told one of his men to build up the fire in the hearth. ''E ain't never gonna ferget me.'

Thomas could hear Zeb well enough, but it took a few moments for his vision to come back. 'At least let my wife go into her room,' he said. 'She's done nothing to you.'

Zeb laughed and looked at Helen. 'She's a pretty bit of fluff, ain't she?' He walked over to where she lay huddled against the wall and pulled her to her feet. 'Mighty womanish!' he exclaimed.

'If you touch her —'

One of Zeb's companions jammed the business end of a gun into his back with such force that he cried out in pain.

'Now I 'old a full 'ouse.' Zeb laughed and reached up to the top of Helen's gown and tore it down the front, exposing her breasts and sex.

'I'll kill you!' Thomas shouted and rushed at Zeb. He never made it. The other two men caught him before he had moved a yard.

'Tie de son-of-a-bitch up,' Zeb ordered. 'I want 'im to watch.'

Thomas was quickly tied to a chair. He glared at Zeb. 'Rape is a hanging offense,' he said.

Zeb pushed the gown off Helen, leaving her completely naked. 'She don't have much in de way of tits,' he said.

Thomas tried to free himself, but couldn't budge the rope that held him. 'I'll kill you, Zeb,' he said in a low voice. 'I'll kill you!'

'You'll 'ave to find me,' Zeb answered. 'But don't you fret none, I ain't goin' to rape your wife. An' my boys won't do not'in' exce't look and maybe touch 'er a bit, but t'at ain't as bad as gettin' raped, now is it?'

Zeb pushed Helen forward. She was too frightened to cry out. What was taking place couldn't actually be happening. It was too horrible to be real!

'Get dat fire nice an' 'ot,' Zeb said.

'It's 'ot now,' his companion said.

Zeb went to the fireplace and took out his hunting knife. 'Looks like you're right,' he said, and he held the blade in the fire until the metal turned cherry red.

'Take 'old of the woman,' he told his companions. 'An' bring 'er 'ere.'

Helen was dragged in front of the hearth and set down on the floor.

'Seen dis done by Cheyennes a couple of time,' Zeb said. He withdrew the red glowing blade from the fire and held it up for Thomas to see. 'I figure each time ya look at 'er, you'll remember me.'

'No!' Thomas screamed. 'For the love of God no! Kill me! Kill me!'

Zeb shook his head and grinned at him. 'I like de Cheyenne way better,' he said, and, turning to Helen, pressed the red point against her cheek.

She screamed and jerked her head away. The sharp stink of burnt flesh filled the air.

Zeb grabbed hold of her hair and pulled it back, then he straddled her naked body and cut her along the right side of her neck.

Helen screamed and then was silent.

'She passed out,' Zeb explained, standing up and moving aside. 'Jest left my mark on 'er an' cut 'er muscle to make 'er 'ead flop to one side. She'll look kinda funny till you get used to it.'

Thomas swallowed huge gulps of air. To shout was useless. It was done. But someday he would get Zeb and butcher him like a pig. Make him bleed slow.

'All right,' Zeb told his two companions, 'you can 'ave 'er now. But no rape, that's a hangin' offense.'

The two men laughed and carried Helen into the bedroom.

'I tol' ya I'd pay ya back,' Zeb said. 'I tol' ya.'

Thomas didn't answer. He closed his eyes and waited for the two men to come out of the bedroom. Finally the first one did. 'You know what,' he said to Zeb, 'she'd been 'ad before.'

Zeb laughed. 'Now ain't dat somet'in'! Seems like you like whores so much you even married one.'

After a while the second man came out. 'She came to,' he said, 'while I was doin' it. I 'ad to clout 'er again.'

'Well, boys,' Zeb said, 'I guess we can leave now dat I've paid my respects.'

'Ain't you goin' to 'ave a try at 'er?' one of the men asked Zeb.

'I already 'ad my fun,' he answered. And then he cut the ropes that bound Thomas. 'Better see to ya wife,' he said, and he motioned his companions toward the door.

'What if he follows —'

"E won't,' Zeb said. "E's got to take care of 'is wife.' And he backed out of the door.

A few moments later Thomas heard the three of them gallop off into the night. Slowly he walked to the door of the bedroom. A shudder passed through his body when he looked at Helen. He bit his lip and immediately tried to bring her to consciousness.

When she opened her eyes and saw him, she began to scream…

ELEVEN

Thomas waited until William and Clem returned to the house before telling anyone about what had happened. He made no mention of the rapes, or that he knew one of the men. He told his father and brother that as far as he could tell the men were just saddle tramps.

'But to mutilate a woman the way they did,' William cried, 'was inhuman.'

Clem agreed.

Thomas stuck to his story no matter how many questions William asked.

'Are you sure they didn't molest her in a sexual way?' William asked.

'No,' Thomas said. 'They just did what you've seen.'

'God,' William exclaimed, 'that was more than enough.' Then he added wistfully, 'She was such a pretty little woman.'

'Her father is going to take this mighty hard,' Clem said.

William agreed and suggested that he and Thomas ride over to the Wicker ranch and tell Sam.

'I'll go alone,' Thomas said. 'She's my wife and —'

'Suit yourself,' William said, and then he told Clem to ride into Paso Diablo for the doctor. He looked at Thomas to see if he had any objections.

'I don't think he can do anything more for her than I have already done,' Thomas said. 'But maybe he can.'

When Sam heard what had happened he turned pale and sat down. He kept shaking his head, and then he looked up at

Thomas and with trembling lips said that he wanted to see his daughter.

It took several weeks for Helen to get back her strength, but she was never the same. Though she remembered having been cut and burned, she could not remember anything else that had happened to her, which was, as far as Thomas was concerned, for the better. He didn't want anyone mixing in his argument with Zeb. He even went so far as to give Sheriff Wyler a false description of the men. But sometimes at night, Helen would wake up screaming, and in her hysterical shouting she would yell Zeb's name over and over again.

Eventually Helen discovered she had been cut and scarred permanently, but she did not become hysterical. Instead she bore her wound with quiet resignation. She accepted what had happened to her as the will of God — His stern rebuke for having sinned with Thomas and for having been so proud, so full of vanity that she thought that she could marry a man who didn't love her and make him love her.

When she told Thomas this, he tried to change her mind. But she clung tenaciously to her belief, and with each passing day became more and more fanatically religious. As her devotion to God grew, the distance between her and Thomas widened.

At first when she lay in bed to recover her health, Thomas was driven by guilt to be attentive and considerate even though he was repelled by the long scar and the way her head flopped over to the right side. But then when Helen took to religion, he found himself detesting her, and angry at himself for feeling that way. William had given him a bellyful of God and now he could expect the same thing from his wife.

To his complete disgust, Thomas discovered Helen would use any excuse not to have sexual relations with him, and when she finally consented she would lie there anxious for him to be done with 'this filthy business,' as she called it. Physical pleasure had become a sin for her, and the only reason she endured it was to become pregnant.

The more Helen denied him, the fiercer became his desire. Not because he wanted her so much, but rather it was the only way he had to assuage his own torment and satisfy his lust. Life became a living hell for Thomas, and arguments between him and Helen were frequent and violent.

Then one night she refused when he wanted her.

Thomas became angry. He told her what he thought about her God. 'I tried,' he shouted, 'to be a husband to you. But you want a saint and I'm a man. Do you understand? I'm a man!'

'You're no better than an animal,' she yelled back. 'A filthy animal who wants only to rut.'

'And you're not even a woman!' he shot back.

'You don't want a woman —'

'Not one like you.'

'No,' she cried. 'Not one like me. What you want — and always wanted — was that whore in Paso Diablo.'

'At least she gives a man his money's worth,' he shouted.

'Then by the living God,' she screamed, 'go to her and leave me in peace. Your idea of love sickens me. Go to her … Go to her…'

Thomas ran from the room and slammed the door behind him. Had he been dressed he would have saddled up and gone to Paso Diablo! Instead he paced back and forth in his nightshirt.

This was one argument he was sure that William and Clem had heard. They couldn't have helped but hear, with all the shouting and yelling that had gone on.

Later, when he was sure Helen was asleep, Thomas returned to his bed. Almost before he knew it he was awake and another day had already started. Then at breakfast Thomas found himself the object of his father's hard-eyed scrutiny.

Ever since Helen had been hurt William had become more silent than ever, though sometimes when they were alone he would ask questions about what had happened. And always Thomas told him the same story, but he soon realized the old man didn't believe it — at least not the part about him not knowing who was responsible for the deed.

As soon as he finished eating Thomas went to the stable to saddle Gray for the day's work, and William followed him.

'I want to talk to you,' his father said, catching up to Thomas before he was halfway across the yard.

'What about?' Thomas asked, continuing to walk.

'I think you know,' William said.

'I don't want to —'

'Will you stop!' William exclaimed. He was rapidly losing patience with Thomas, and his son's abuse of Helen was hurrying his feelings along. There was no doubt in William's mind that he felt closer to Helen than to Thomas.

'There's nothing to talk about,' Thomas answered, meeting the old man's steely eyes without flinching.

'She's a good woman,' William said. 'Better than you deserve.'

'In your eyes,' Thomas told him, 'but hardly in bed.'

'Is that all you think about?'

Thomas shook his head. 'No,' he replied. 'Sometimes I think how damn foolish I was not to have hightailed it out of here when I had the chance.'

'Have you been seeing that woman in Paso Diablo?' William growled.

'What I do or don't do, Father, is none of your damn business,' Thomas answered flatly. 'And what's more,' he added, 'don't make it any of your business.'

'Is that a warning?'

Thomas shrugged. 'You wanted me married so I'm married,' he said. 'For better or for worse, eh? Well, let me tell you, Father, it was for the worse. Not that you really care. You got yourself a Bible-reading, Bible-believing daughter-in-law out of it. But I didn't get a thing. '

'Are you blaming her for what happened?'

Thomas shook his head. 'I blame myself,' he said sharply. 'I took my gun off to get married —'

'Women and killing are all you ever think about.'

'You forgot whiskey, Father,' Thomas told him. 'The best trio a man ever had: women, whiskey, and fighting. Now leave me be. I had enough for one morning.' And he stalked off to the stable.

'Thomas?' William called. But his son paid no heed. Slowly he turned around and looked at the house and saw Clem standing near the door. William heaved a deep sigh of despair and started for the bunkhouse.

'You'll never reach him that way,' Clem said, falling in beside his father.

'You heard?'

'Most of it,' Clem said.

'Do you think Helen heard?'

'No,' he said, 'she's in the kitchen. Besides, I closed the front door.'

William stopped. 'What's wrong with him?' he asked, looking at his middle son.

'Angry,' Clem answered, 'and full of hate.'

'For his wife and his father,' William said.

'And for himself,' Clem nodded.

William snorted. 'He's too damn proud of his gun and his way with women to hate himself,' he said.

'I don't see it that way,' Clem said. 'Fate — or God, if you will — played a foul trick on him. He didn't want to marry Helen in the first place.'

'So you're taking his side, is that it?'

'I'm not taking anyone's side,' Clem told him. 'And I don't think you should either. Remember,' he said, 'it was Helen who drove him out of her bed, not the other way around.'

'A marriage is more than that.'

'Possibly,' Clem responded. 'But Thomas is too young to put down the demands of his flesh.'

'I will not stand for him chasing after that Mex whore!'

'Don't push him, Father,' Clem cautioned.

'Seems to me that he's the one who's doing all the pushing.'

'Put yourself in Thomas' boots and see if it still seems that way.'

'Bah!' William exclaimed. Then he added, 'I've never seen a mustang that couldn't be broken.'

Clem nodded, but then said, 'Thomas isn't a mustang, he's a man.'

'All the more reason, then, for him to see the light and get used to the bridle that God meant all men to wear.'

'You're going to force his hand.'

William stopped. 'What does that mean?' he asked, looking at his son.

'With a man like Thomas it could mean anything,' Clem answered. 'But I do know that if you try to saddle him any more than he's already saddled, he'll buck all the more. He won't stand for it.'

'I guess,' the old man said, rubbing his grizzled chin, 'the Almighty meant it to be that way. But let me tell you this. I'd rather see him in hell first than let him bring down any more pain on Helen's shoulders. And by the living God I mean that!'

'He's your son,' Clem told him.

William snorted. 'That doesn't give him any special privileges,' he said. 'He owes that woman something and he's going to pay his debt.'

'What about what he owes himself?'

'I'm not interested in that,' the old man said. 'He's got more than most men. If he can't be satisfied with what he has, he's at fault and no one else.' He turned and walked away, leaving Clem behind him.

By early September, the rains that had given life to vast stretches of range land in the spring seemed never to have fallen. Day after day the sky was an eye-shattering brilliant blue. It rose to a big yellow ball, and when it set the ball was blood red.

The grass withered and died. The waterholes dried up and the creeks and streams were turned into sun-baked gulches. The ever-present wind was hot and dry.

The lack of water and the heat took a heavy toll on the cattle. Most of the calves born that spring died. Their bodies swelled up and stank. Only the buzzards and the coyotes flourished.

Each day that passed for the men who rode the range was a day spent in hell. They were red-eyed, thirsty, and as touchy as the cattle they tended. Arguments were frequent and fist-fights common. Even the best of friends found something to quarrel about.

And when the land became dry enough, the wind picked up bits of it, until everything and everyone was covered with a fine yellow dust. Then men covered their mouths and noses with their wipes, but somehow the dust got through and they breathed it into their lungs and felt its grittiness in their mouths. Their food was covered with it and the water they drank was cloudy with it.

Every Sunday the people in church prayed for rain, pleading with the Almighty to relieve their suffering. But rain did not come. The fine yellow dust gathered into large clouds that changed the color of the sky from blue to yellow and then to brown for days on end. And when the dust storm passed, the sky was eye-scalding blue again.

In all the years that William had been in the country he had never experienced such a summer. He was forced to kill off almost a thousand head of cattle so that the others would survive. Nothing seemed right! And the situation in his own house between Thomas and Helen only served to underscore the other difficulties.

He seldom spoke to Thomas, and when he did it was only about the herd. As for Clem, he didn't have much to say to him either.

Helen was really the only one with whom he felt comfortable. She was willing to listen to his comments about the weather or anything else. And when Sunday came she went to church with him while his two sons lazed about the house. Clem slept most of the day away while Thomas spent it drinking.

With each day that passed, William became more and more convinced that God was punishing the people for some transgression, and he racked his brain to discover the sin that had brought the wrath of the Almighty down on them.

Then, one evening during dinner, he spoke to Helen about it, with the hope that she might be able to help him find the cause of God's anger.

'No such thing,' Thomas said, before his wife could answer.

William looked at his son. The boy's eyes were red-rimmed and bloodshot. His face was the color of dried leather and his chin was dark with the bristle of several days' growth.

'It has nothing to do with God,' Thomas said.

'God is —'

A short burst of laughter from Thomas cut him short. 'Old man,' he said, 'the heat has cooked your brains.'

William's jaw tightened. 'I'm not looking to argue with you,' he said.

'Then don't make stupid statements,' Thomas shot back. 'What's happening here has as much to do with God as I have to do with my wife.'

Helen gasped. It wasn't true. After the last argument she had let him use her body. She shook her head and began to sob.

'Haven't you *any* feelings for her?' William asked. He left his chair and, going behind Helen, he placed his hands on her drooping shoulders. 'Pay him no heed,' he told her. 'If anyone's brains are fried, it's his.'

Again Thomas laughed.

Suddenly William realized his son was drunk, and that made him angry. He couldn't stop him from drinking on Sunday, but during the week a man worked and didn't spend his time with a bottle. 'You're drunk,' he said.

'Not nearly as drunk as I'd like to be,' Thomas answered.

'Leave the table!' William ordered. 'I won't stand for a man being drunk at my table, not even if he's my own son.'

'Pa,' Clem said, 'leave it alone.'

William glared at him. 'I'm still the head of this house,' he said. 'And I told him to leave the table.'

For a moment Thomas hesitated. Whatever fuzziness had been in his brain was obliterated by the sudden surge of anger that rushed through him.

'I'm waiting for you to leave,' William challenged.

Thomas looked at his father and then at his wife.

'Please,' Helen cried, turning her face up to William, 'don't make him go!'

But William shook his head. Even if he wanted to back down, it was not in his nature to. Once he said something he meant it.

Thomas stood up, walked into the bedroom, and dug out the box containing the shawl he had bought in Christi. Then he reappeared and went to the open door.

'Will the two of you stop it?' Clem said.

Thomas didn't even glance back over his shoulder.

'Clem, for God sakes, stop him!' Helen cried. She knew exactly where he was going.

'You go after him,' Clem answered. 'He's your husband.'

'He won't listen to me,' she wailed. 'He won't listen.'

'Make him listen!' Clem shouted.

Thomas heard everything, but none of it bothered him. The time had come for him to act. No longer could he, or did he want to, push Lisa out of his mind. He saddled Gray and rode slowly out of the front yard.

'Thomas,' Helen shouted from the doorway, 'don't go! I'm begging you not to go.'

He looked straight ahead.

'Thomas,' she cried, 'you can't do this to me.'

He rode past the house and turned toward the gate.

Helen ran after him. 'Thomas,' she yelled, 'Thomas, I'm pregnant. I'm carrying your child. Do you hear me? Oh, Thomas, come back!'

He reined in, turned and looked at her. 'Go back to the house,' he told her.

She came alongside of him. 'I'm going to have a baby,' she said, looking up at him. 'Doesn't that mean anything to you?'

'Nothing,' he answered.

'You can't mean it!' She grabbed hold of his leg.

'Nothing,' he answered. 'You mean nothing, the child means nothing … even I mean nothing.'

Helen let go of his leg. 'And you think that whore means something?' she cried up at him.

'Go back to the house,' he said.

'Oh, God,' she cried. 'God, hear my plea.' And she dropped to her knees. 'Strike her dead!' Helen shouted. 'Strike his whore dead!'

'Go back to the house,' Thomas told her, and he touched Gray's flanks with his legs. Instantly the animal started to move.

'I'll never forgive you!' Helen called after him.

'And I will never ask for it,' Thomas shouted back as he quickened Gray's pace.

Thomas rode slowly toward Paso Diablo. There was no need for him to hurry. He knew Lisa would be at the Broken Horn. It wouldn't even matter if she was upstairs with another man. Thomas would wait.

For the first time in months Thomas felt he was riding toward something he wanted, not something that William wanted for him. The old man would have to swallow crow. He might not like its taste but he would not spit it out, especially now that he knew that Helen was pregnant.

Thomas smiled and patted Gray's neck. He could see a certain amount of irony in his present situation. By holding the threat of banishment over Thomas, William had forced him into an unwilling marriage. But as things stood, the old man couldn't exercise his power because the marriage had given Thomas the legal right to a portion of the land and the livestock on it. And the child that Helen was carrying gave him a cudgel to use on his father should the old man suddenly take it in his mind to oppose him. Thomas knew it was a lousy way to think about the child he had spawned, and maybe, if there were a God, he'd be damned for it. But to pretend, even to himself, that he had any other feelings about the child would have gone against his own idea of what was right and what was wrong.

Even though the sun was close to the western horizon, the heat was so intense that the land seemed to heave up and buck like a bronc who feels the weight of the saddle for the first time and doesn't like it. Thomas scanned the sky for some tell-tale sign that rain would soon fall. But there was none. It was clear. And in the east, where the daylight had already faded, a few diamond-hard stars were already visible.

When he rounded the knoll that stood above Paso Diablo, Thomas slowed Gray down to a walk. Up until he came in sight of the town he had not thought about Lisa in any way other than to imagine her in his arms again. That vision was enough to sustain his deep, hungry longing for her.

As he swung up Main Street, Thomas realized that Lisa had good reason to tell him to go to hell. The last time they had been together he had run from her, and he remembered how she had stood at the window on the day of his wedding and looked down at him. Though he was too far away from her to see her tears, he knew from the expression on her face that she was crying. But she should have known that he had not been happy either.

Damn it, she should have known!

Thomas guided Gray up to the hitching bar in front of the Broken Horn. Tiny was standing off to the right of the swinging doors. He was cooling himself with a makeshift fan that had once been a page in a newspaper.

'Any sign of rain?' the barkeep asked.

'None,' Thomas answered as he swung out of the saddle.

'Seems like the whole county's about to burn up,' Tiny commented. 'How's the water down your way?'

'Scarce, and turning more alkaline every day.'

'Same story all over,' Tiny said.

Thomas finished tethering Gray and walked up the wooden steps. 'Lisa here?' he asked.

The barkeep squinted at him.

'Well, is she or —'

'She's here,' Tiny said.

Thomas took a deep breath. The words came hard to him. He let the air out of his lungs and finally asked, 'Alone?'

Tiny nodded.

Thomas returned the gesture and started through the swinging doors.

'You aimin' to start with her again?'

The question caught Thomas off guard. It wasn't the kind of thing Tiny would ask. He had been tending bar long enough to know better than to mix in other people's business. But Thomas liked him well enough to answer. 'I kept away as long as I could,' he said, and then in a much lower voice added, 'I should have come a long time ago.'

The barkeep didn't say anything more, and Thomas walked through the swinging doors. He stopped for a moment to let his eyes adjust to the dim light. Then he looked around. Two men were at a table on the far side of the room playing cards. A third man was at the bar. Then he saw Lisa. She was off to the right near the window. Thomas wondered if she had seen him ride in.

When he started toward her, she turned and faced him. Less than an arm's length from her Thomas stopped.

Neither of them spoke. Each waited for the other to say something that would breach the distance between them. Words? Perhaps. But not at that moment.

Even if Lisa wanted to speak, she would have found her throat too dry and her lips too parched. The moment she had seen Thomas riding up the street she had known that he had come for her. She looked straight at him. His face was sweaty and streaked with dust, like the faces of the other men who took her upstairs. But his eyes and mouth were different. There was sadness in his eyes, and his cracked lips were narrowed with determination.

'You know why I have come,' Thomas said in a whisper.

She nodded.

'We will go to your place,' he said, reaching for her.

Lisa drew back. *Tienes un mujer,*' she told him.

'I love you,' he answered.

Her eyes filled with tears. 'No,' she said. 'I am for sale, but not for you.'

He nodded. 'I've missed you,' he told her.

She shook her head.

'Lisa,' he said, 'I love you. I had to marry. But now it's different.' And he took hold of her arms and pulled her to him.

She struggled to free herself. Then his lips found hers. The hurt and anger she felt oozed out of her body.

'Come,' he said, moving his lips from hers. 'Come with me.'

'*Sí,*' she said. 'I am yours.'

Thomas held her hand and together they walked toward the swinging door. 'Lisa won't be back tonight,' Thomas told the barkeep.

'Didn't think she would,' Tiny answered, still fanning himself.

TWELVE

The months of heat and drought were brought to a swift end by a thunderstorm of gigantic proportions. By the time the chill of fall set in, Clem had returned to his studies in the East. Thomas was sorry to see him leave. He felt more alone than ever, and even his frequent visits to Lisa didn't change this feeling.

In a few short weeks Thomas gathered about him a number of young men who seemed to have no other purpose in life but to raise hell. He worked as he had before, but when he was free he went to Paso Diablo. He drank more than he had before, and when he was in town he spent more time gambling than he previously had.

Sam Wicker rode into town as soon as he found out that Thomas had taken up with Lisa again. He came into the Broken Horn and went directly to the table where his son-in-law was playing cards.

'Is it true?' he asked sharply.

The other men at the table started to move away.

'No need for that,' Thomas told his companions. Then he looked up at his father-in-law. 'Is what true?'

'Stop playing cat and mouse with me,' Sam replied angrily. 'I want to know whether you've taken up with that Mex whore again.'

'Yes,' Thomas answered, and he asked the dealer for two more cards.

'Is that all you have to say?' Sam shouted.

'That's all,' Thomas answered.

'And what about my daughter?'

Thomas shrugged.

'Doesn't it make any difference to you that she's carrying your child?'

'No,' Thomas said looking up at Sam's livid face. 'I guess if it did I would be with her and not here.'

Sam shook his head. 'I was a fool to let her marry you,' he said.

'And I was a fool to marry her,' Thomas answered. 'That makes each of us a fool. Now don't be a fool again and say or try something —'

'Some day,' Sam told him, 'someday you'll get what's coming to you, and with God's help I'll be there —'

'Maybe,' Thomas answered. 'Maybe.' And he screwed his eyes up toward his father-in-law. 'But I hardly doubt that God is interested in your daughter or me. I should think he has more important things to consider. Now if you'll stop your jabbering I will go back to my game.'

Sam sputtered for a few moments and then stomped out of the Broken Horn.

Thomas looked at the other men at the table and said, 'I don't think I'll be welcome at his table anymore.' His comment drew laughter and then the game continued.

Though Sam didn't see Lisa, she saw and heard him. Thomas had not told her that Helen was pregnant. Lisa was furious with him. That same night she demanded that he leave Helen and live with her permanently.

'No,' he answered. 'I told you no more times than I can count.'

'It is because of the child?'

'No,' Thomas shouted. 'I want what's mine. Do you understand that?' He smashed his fist down on the table. 'My blood and my sweat are in that land. I was just a kid when I started to work ... my father made me ride before I learned to read or write.'

'You want too much,' Lisa shouted back. 'You want me, your wife, your child, the ranch — what else do you want?'

'Just to be left alone,' he roared back at her. 'Just to be left alone, you whoring bitch!'

'And who made me a whore?' Lisa screamed. 'Who did that, Thomas?'

He could not take that from her. Her words cut him deeply. But she spoke the truth. Each time he made love to her he thought about the other men who loosed their passion into her.

'I can't take it,' he told her. 'I can't have you pulling on me.' And he ran from the shanty. A few moments later he was on Gray.

But Lisa rushed after him. 'Next time you want to fuck me,' she yelled, 'I will make you pay just like the others.'

Thomas got halfway to the ranch before he realized how hard he had ridden Gray. Then he stopped. He couldn't go back to the ranch and leave Lisa full of hate and anger. He turned his mount around and went slowly back to Paso Diablo.

Though he loved Lisa, much of the time he spent with her was stormy. The only times that she didn't tear at him were when they made love. But more and more Thomas' movements between the ranch and Lisa depended on where he could find a few days' peace. When he was away from Lisa, he missed her. But when he stayed at the ranch for any length of time he felt weighed down by his father's silence and his wife's silent forgiving attitude. He would have preferred Helen to lash out at him for his profligacy, but true to her religious fanaticism, she turned the other cheek, or maybe the fight had gone out of her.

Thomas realized in a few months that he had moved from one kind of hell into another. There didn't seem to be any way out for him. He felt as though he were rushing headlong toward some far greater violence than he could possibly imagine. Maybe it was because there was so much talk about the coming war.

It almost seemed as though somewhere out on the range, beyond where the eye could see, the war was waiting. Just sitting there waiting!

Even if it wasn't out there, the men at the Broken Horn talked about it as though it were — and that made it almost real. Men spoke about their willingness to die for their beliefs; they spoke about southern honor as though it were something unique from all other kinds of honor; and they spoke about the God-given right for them to own slaves.

There was a tension, a kind of muscular ripple that quivered in the air whenever men gathered to talk about the war.

Thomas remembered what Clem had said about making a choice. He still had not made his, but he began to feel that he would have to make one soon, very soon.

Late in March of 1861, Helen's time had come. He was at the ranch when it happened. Maria acted as midwife, and after eight hours of labor Helen delivered a son.

Thomas should have been a very happy man, but he wasn't. The child had come from a loveless marriage, and though it was part of him he did not want it. Small and helpless as it was, it was another link in a chain that bound him to a woman he did not love.

But William was truly pleased that he had a grandson. In Thomas' presence he stood at Helen's bedside and promised the boy would never want for anything, that he would provide the child with everything.

'That won't be necessary,' Thomas said, angered by his father's gesture. 'I'll give him what he needs.'

'The way you give Helen?' William questioned hotly.

'What I do or don't do for my wife,' Thomas said, 'is none of your business.'

Helen shook her head. 'Must you argue even at my bedside?' she asked, looking up at Thomas.

'I don't want him mixing in my life.'

'Seems like you need someone to mix in it,' William answered, 'since you're damn near wrecking it.'

Rather than answer his father he knew a better way of getting back at the old man. 'I want the boy named after my grandfather,' he said, talking to Helen but looking at William.

'You wouldn't do that?' His father paled. 'You wouldn't do that?'

Thomas nodded. 'I never knew him,' he said. 'But I figure since you hate him so much I probably would have liked him, maybe even loved him.'

William's lips trembled. 'You'd do that to me?' he asked.

'Yes,' he answered. Pointing to Helen and the boy, he said, 'I owe you that much for what you have given me.'

'You're no good,' William told him. 'No good to yourself or anyone else.'

'Please,' Helen whimpered. 'Please don't. I'll do anything you want, Thomas, but don't argue now.'

'Name him Ethan,' he said sharply. 'That's all I want.' And he started to leave the room.

'Where are you going?' Helen asked.

'To celebrate the birth of Ethan Carey, my son. How about it, Father, will you drink to Ethan with me?'

William hesitated.

'Go with him,' Helen whispered.

'All right,' the old man said with a nod. 'I'll drink to your son.'

'Call him by his name, Father, or does it stick in your throat?'

William didn't answer.

After the birth of his son, Thomas remained at the ranch. Several times he caught himself thinking about the boy, wondering about him, trying to see into the distant future when the boy would be old enough to ride, to shoot a gun, to understand something about the relationship between his mother and father. Notwithstanding his initial reaction to the child and that he had named him to spite William, he could not truly deny the blood tie that existed between them. And when he was sure that neither his father nor Helen saw him, he'd go into the bedroom and silently look at the infant. Several times he extended his forefinger toward the boy and felt a peculiar thrill when his son's small hand touched him.

'Ethan,' he whispered one afternoon as he stood by the cradle, 'you picked yourself a bad hand when you picked me for your father.'

'It was God's choice,' Helen said. She had been standing in the doorway watching, but when he spoke she felt she had to answer.

Thomas faced her. He was caught off guard and flushed deeply.

'I think he's beginning to look like you,' she said, coming into the room and taking her place next to him. 'He has your eyes and your chin.'

'I hope he has more sense than I have,' Thomas said. He was amazed how easily Helen spoke to him about the child. He wondered if she had seen him the other times he had come to look at the boy.

Helen raised her eyes from the infant and looked at Thomas. 'There'd be two of us to love you now,' she said.

Thomas moved back.

'I know I can't stop you from going to Paso Diablo,' she whispered, 'but he will need you.'

Already the link was being closed, but he couldn't be angry, especially since he realized she was telling him what he already knew.

She pushed her blonde hair back and revealed the scar.

The sight of it made Thomas' stomach tighten. It was bad enough to have to look at her head lolled over to one side, but to have to see the scar was too much. He shook his head. 'It won't ever work for us,' he told her. 'At least not the way you want.'

She nodded and her long hair fell over the scar, hiding it from view. 'I have no more anger in me, Thomas,' she told him quietly. 'This is your home, Ethan is your son. You are free to come and go as you choose. I know now that I was wrong and you were right about our marriage, but I've made peace with myself about it. I can't be the kind of woman you think you want, but you have no cause to punish the child because of what I did. He is innocent.'

Thomas sighed wearily. 'It was as much my fault as yours,' he said, 'especially that afternoon on the hill.' Helen flushed. 'I don't want to argue with you,' he told her, 'but I can't be what you and my father want me to be.'

She nodded. 'I will have to be content, then, with whatever you are,' she replied, and then fell silent, hoping that he would see the expression of her sorrow and hope deep in her eyes, and in the lines that had come early to her young face.

Thomas would have reached for her, taken her in his arms, if for no other reason than to show his appreciation, to indicate that he too was tired of arguing and that he really did want to thank her for —

His thoughts and movements were stopped by the sudden sound of yelling riders galloping into the front yard. He rushed out of the bedroom and Helen followed.

William was already at the open door.

'The war,' one of the men shouted. 'It's come. Fort Sumter was captured by General Beauregard. The war has started … c'mon, Thomas, we've got us a war to fight now!' And he gave a wild yell.

'God help us!' William exclaimed.

'Saddle up, Thomas,' came another yell from the half-dozen riders. 'We don't want to miss any of the shooting.'

Thomas looked at Helen. She said nothing and made no movement.

'Hurry!' a third man urged. 'Hurry. We've got to round up the other men.'

Thomas started out of the door.

'Where are you going?' his father asked.

'For a ride,' Thomas answered. 'For a ride from nowhere to nowhere.'

'But you don't even believe —'

Thomas pushed past his father, and a few minutes later he was in the saddle. The choice proved to be easy. He was called and he answered. That was all there was to it. Maybe he knew all the time what he would and what he would not do. Maybe it was the one way for him to get away from his life. Maybe he wanted to die and that was why he chose to go to war. It was as good a reason as any, probably even better than most, since he didn't believe in or make a lot of noise about the South and her honor, or whatever else the others thought they would be fighting for.

Thomas waved his sombrero at his wife and father and then galloped away.

'It will be a while before he leaves,' William said, turning to face Helen.

'But he will not spend it here,' she stated. 'This happened just when…' She shook her head, broke off and ran into the bedroom, where she threw herself down on the bed and wept.

William quietly closed the bedroom door. Then he took his pipe, filled and lit it. When he was satisfied with the way it was drawing, he went to the front door. It was still open and he leaned against one side of the passageway to look out across the range. In the distance the mountains were already blue-gray from the coming twilight.

Something needed thinking about, something that had lain hidden in William's brain until Thomas had named his son Ethan. That one act above all the others had made him see his son as another Ishmael, the spawn of Hagar, and not his own.

What Thomas had said about his grandfather had been the blind truth. They would have loved each other. They would have recognized that there was something more than just blood between them. Thomas, like his grandfather, belonged nowhere and to no one on God's green earth.

But now that the war had come Thomas might be denied all the years his grandfather had had. Thomas might not come back, and this was what William thought about.

There was little doubt in his mind that the good Lord would be doing them all a service if He took Thomas to Him. The boy was hardly a husband to Helen, and she would be better off without him. William doubted that his son would prove to be much of a father, and he was damn little comfort to him as a son!

William bit down so hard on the stem of his pipe that a sudden slash of pain cut across his jaw muscles, making him wince. But he wouldn't let go. The pain was beautiful, a kind of pleasure.

If he could have only been sure that Thomas would not come back, then maybe he would be able to raise his grandson the way he should have raised his son. If only William could have been sure that his son would die, then maybe he would be able to be happy.

The pain in his jaw transcended pleasure. He was forced to release his hold on the pipe. At the same time, he turned and went into the house. He did not for a moment doubt the righteousness of his thoughts. Even the Bible stated, 'If thine eye offends thee, pluck it out.' Surely Thomas offended him, vexed him to the extreme limits of endurance as a man and a father.

He paused for a moment outside of the bedroom where Helen lay weeping. The war, William thought, might rid her of Thomas, and then again it might not. The good die young, but men like Thomas had a tenacious hold of life; somehow they always managed to survive.

The war couldn't be trusted, at least not as far as Thomas was concerned. Another way would have to be found, one that would be foolproof.

William went to the fireplace and knocked the ashes from his pipe. He felt better than he had in a long time. He sat down and, staring at the flames in the hearth, whispered, 'The Lord giveth and the Lord taketh away, blessed be the name of the Lord.'

THIRTEEN

The line of men and horses twisted through the heavily misted woods. They moved slowly, almost noiselessly. The length of the column and its numerous snake-like twists prevented all but the first troopers from seeing the back of the man at its head. And even those men who rode close behind Lieutenant Thomas Carey did not pay much attention to him, not out of disrespect but because they were weary and saddle-sore from the three days they had spent on patrol.

Thomas slouched forward. His hands rested on the saddle horn and his strong arms provided a double buttress against his body making any additional movement impossible.

The desire to close his eyes and doze was almost overwhelming, but he willed himself to remain awake. The men in the troop, some of whom were from Paso Diablo, trusted him to lead them back to the bivouac area without stumbling into a fight with a Yankee patrol. So far they had been lucky and had not seen one bluecoat during the entire time they had been out. But they were still several hours away from their home base, and Thomas knew from experience that there were many enemy patrols moving about. He didn't have to see them to know they were there.

The pre-dawn darkness gave way to the dull light of day and the mist turned into a mizzling rain. Thomas shifted his position in the saddle and flipped up the broad collar of his coat. If he had come to hate anything during the months he had been in the army, it had to be the weather. It seemed to him that the rain, the snow and the bitter cold were far more troublesome than the Yankees.

He raised his eyes and looked at the trees on either side of him. Their leaves were already turning and it was only the middle of October, or was it early November? Thomas found it difficult to keep track of the days and the months. Time had little relevancy. A minute in combat could seem like hours, just as the past three days seemed like weeks.

Thomas slouched forward again. He let his thoughts race ahead several hours to when he would be out of the saddle and hunker down close to a fire, drink hot coffee, maybe even sleep for a few hours.

Sergeant Josiah Whipple rode directly behind Thomas. He was a big raw-boned man who came from Georgia. He had been with the troop before Thomas took command of it. At first he didn't think much of the new lieutenant, if for no other reason than his age. Like so many other young men who bought their commissions, the lieutenant looked very good on parade, but Whipple doubted that he would be able to stay alive in battle, let alone be responsible for the lives of other men. But the first time the lieutenant led the men into action Whipple was quick to realize he had been mistaken about him. The lieutenant was calm and deadly under fire. That first blooding seemed to have happened so long ago that Whipple could not remember where it had taken place, and the other battles and skirmishes that followed forged a bond of friendship and respect between himself and the lieutenant. It was the kind of thing that could only happen in war, when men shared each other's lives and, if necessary, each other's deaths.

To ease the ache between his shoulders, Thomas straightened up, then he rubbed his eyes. A moment later he glanced back at the troop. The few men he saw were hard, grim-looking veterans, who were experts in the bloody business of killing. He faced front again and wondered if any of them were disappointed that the patrol had not encountered any blue-bellies? Probably. Thomas knew there was a breed of men who enjoyed killing just the way some men enjoyed making love to many different women. The war gave them the opportunity to kill without worrying about the consequences. As far as Thomas was concerned, he had already done enough killing. It was one thing to throw down with a man who gave you cause, but it was something else again to gun down or saber a man you didn't even know.

For a moment he wondered how William might explain why one kind of killing was considered wrong and the other right? Then bracing himself against the saddle horn, he slouched forward again and went back to thinking about the warmth of the fire and the hot coffee he would have once he was back at the base camp.

Off to the left of the column, concealed by the thick undergrowth of the woods, a lone man followed its slow progress. He had picked up its trail shortly after the troop had left the bivouac area, and for the past three days he had never let it get more than a hundred yards away from him. At night during the brief time the column rested, he moved in even closer. And though he could have killed any one of the troopers — maybe even more than one — he did not. The years he had spent with the Cheyennes gave him a zest for stalking.

But the time was rapidly approaching when he would kill one of them, though it wouldn't be the one he had come to kill. That would come later. Now the game was to make him sweat.

The man smiled and rubbed his unshaven chin. The idea of playing cat-and-mouse pleased him. Sooner or later he knew his victim would figure out what was happening, but by then it wouldn't do him much good except to make him jumpy. The jumpier he got the easier it would be to kill him.

Again the man smiled. Then suddenly he realized that the troop had halted. He dropped to his stomach, and at the same time fitted the rifle butt to his shoulder. He watched the movement of the lieutenant and then, sighting down the long barrel of the Sharp's rifle, slowly drew bead on the officer. He could have killed him then, but that would have ended the game too soon. He eased the rifle slightly to the right and sighted his new target.

'What's wrong?' Whipple questioned softly, the instant after he saw the lieutenant hand signal to halt.

'Not sure,' Thomas answered, turning half around. He had seen nothing to make him wary, but some inner sense told him that danger was very close. His whole body tingled with excitement. Thomas knew he couldn't explain the feeling and he didn't try.

'Ya think Yankees'd come in so close?'

'Might,' Thomas replied, 'if they didn't figure we'd be here.'

'Up ahead?'

'Could be,' he said. 'These trees offer good cover. I wouldn't want to get caught in a line of crossfire.'

Whipple nodded.

'Better send the scouts —'

The report of a single shot filled the woods.

Instantly Thomas' mount reared up. But even as he brought the animal under control, Whipple pitched backwards and fell to the ground. His mount started to break from the column.

'Get that horse!' Thomas shouted. Two men started after it, and in a matter of moments they brought it back. 'Troop dismount!' he ordered. 'Prepare to fight on foot. Use the nearest cover.'

He swung out of the saddle, handed the reins of his mount to the closest man and bent down to Whipple. Gently Thomas rolled him over. Blood was pouring out of the man's throat. His eyes were glazed.

A moment later his head lolled off to the left. He was dead.

Thomas stood up, momentarily expecting to engage the enemy. But the woods were silent, except for the soft patter of the rain as it fell on the autumn leaves.

As soon as Thomas returned to the bivouac area he made his report to Captain Grayson, the company commander. Once the basic military facts were covered, Thomas concluded his explanation of the patrol's activities with an account of Sergeant Whipple's death.

'Did you search for the sniper?' the captain asked, looking up at Thomas from the other side of the desk.

'No, sir.'

'Then could you be sure that there wasn't more than one Yankee?' Grayson questioned.

'There was only one shot fired,' Thomas explained. 'My guess —'

'I am not interested in your guess, lieutenant,' Grayson said tersely. 'The point is that with a little effort on your part, you could have made sure that there was only one man.'

'I don't think so,' Thomas commented. 'There was no way of telling from where the shot was fired.' He was not about to give an inch to the small red-headed man who glared up at him from behind his desk.

Grayson placed his palms down on the field desk and, pushing down on them, stood up. He was a short, wiry man with copper-colored hair and a freckled face. He was devoted to duty. Though he was a strict disciplinarian, he was more concerned about the welfare of his men than a great many other commanders.

'Sergeant Whipple was a good man,' Grayson said. 'He served with this battalion since Shiloh.'

'No one knows that better than I do.'

The captain snorted. 'I should think, then, you would have made some effort to find the man who killed him.'

'As I have already told you, sir, I had the men dismount and—'

'Not again, lieutenant,' Grayson said, holding up his hand. 'Spare me your excuses.'

'Yes, sir.'

Grayson moved off to one side of the tent. 'Has it occurred to you,' he questioned, 'that you could have been the one who was shot?'

'Yes, sir.'

'Has it also occurred to you that the sniper chose to shoot at a sergeant when it would have been just as easy for him to have killed a lieutenant?'

Thomas hesitated. He became conscious of the sound of the rain striking the heavy canvas of the tent.

'I asked a question, lieutenant, and I want an answer.'

'I had not thought about it that way,' Thomas replied.

'What made you halt the column?' Grayson snapped, stepping back to the desk.

'I had the feeling —'

'That you were being watched?'

'Yes. if you want to put it that way, sir.'

'And you didn't order your scouts out?'

'I started to do that when Sergeant Whipple was shot,' Thomas said. He was trying desperately hard not to lose his temper. Grayson was pushing too hard.

'There's more to being a good officer,' Grayson told him, 'than fighting. Sometimes a man must use his brains, must stop and think. Do you understand me?'

'I think so, sir.'

Grayson shook his head. 'Did Sergeant Whipple have any kin?' he asked.

Thomas shook his head. 'I wouldn't know, sir.' Thomas had never asked the man about his family.

Grayson rubbed the corners of his eyes near the bridge of his nose with his thumb and forefinger. Then he asked, 'Have you arranged for a burial detail?'

'Yes, sir.'

The captain nodded. 'Either tomorrow or the next day,' he said, 'we will be getting replacements. No doubt there will be a few sergeants among them. If you have no objections I'll assign one to take Sergeant Whipple's place.'

'I have no objections.'

The captain lifted an envelope from his desk. 'This letter is for you,' he said, handing it across the desk to Thomas.

'Thank you, sir.'

'Remember what I said,' Grayson told him, 'about the sniper's choosing —'

'I am not responsible for Whipple's death!' Thomas exclaimed hotly.

Grayson was too stunned by his junior officer's outburst to make any sort of response. For several moments the two men stood absolutely silent. Then Grayson said, 'That will be all, lieutenant.'

Thomas came to attention, saluted, did an about-face and left the tent. He was too furious to read the letter, and jammed it into his coat pocket. He couldn't believe that Grayson held him responsible for Whipple's death. He clenched his teeth and rapidly made his way to the other side of the bivouac area, where the men from his troop were waiting for him before they buried Whipple.

'Sir, would you care to say somethin'?' Corporal Downs asked.

Thomas took a quick look at the men. From the expressions on their faces, he knew they wanted him to speak. He owed them that much, and surely he owed it to Whipple.

'A good many of us have seen other men die,' he began, and stopped to clear his throat before going on. 'I guess it's something that few of us ever get used to. Sergeant Whipple — the best thing I could say about him was that he was a man.' Thomas raised his eyes and saw the men nod approvingly. 'Maybe a lot more could be said, but the sergeant wasn't one for fuss and feathers about anything or anyone. If any of you men would like to add anything just speak out.'

The troopers remained silent.

'All right,' Thomas said, 'best bury him.'

The four men on the ropes began to pay them out, and the pinewood box sank slowly into the muddy six-by-six hole.

Thomas tossed the first shovelful of earth into the grave and then handed the shovel to the trooper nearest him. One by one the men took their turn filling the grave. When the last man had finished, he handed the shovel back to Thomas, who used it several more times before giving it to one of the men from the burial detail.

A short time after Thomas left the graveside, he hunkered down next to a fire and drank several cups of strong black coffee. The anger he had felt against Grayson gave way to a dark mood of depression.

Thomas shook his head. Then it occurred to him that the sniper had two other opportunities to kill him: when his horse reared and when he dismounted to help Whipple. But the sniper had not fired either time.

Why?

Suddenly Thomas realized that the sniper could have been there to kill Whipple and no one else. If that was the case, then the sniper probably wasn't a Yankee, but someone who had a score to settle with Whipple.

Thomas stood up. The explanation seemed reasonable; at least, it answered the question that Grayson had put to him. He turned and looked at the captain's tent. For a moment he thought about presenting the explanation to Grayson, if for no other reason than to clear himself of the responsibility for Whipple's death. But then Thomas changed his mind. It was enough for him to know what had happened.

He turned and walked slowly to the tent where he was to sleep. A few minutes later Thomas stretched out on the earthen floor and, pulling the coarse blanket over his head, quickly fell asleep.

Tired as he was, Thomas did not sleep soundly. He was aware of the various noises in the bivouac area. The passing of men and horses close to his lean-to and the hourly calling of one guard to the other were part of the familiar rhythm of the camp. But the instant some discordant note penetrated his light sleep, Thomas immediately became tense and alert for action. Motionless, he lay waiting to see what the next few moments would bring. As seconds became minutes, he slowly relaxed and drifted into a demi-slumber once again.

The time he had spent fighting had sharpened his senses, but at the same time it denied him the pleasure of a deep and restful sleep. And in this demi-state of wakefulness, Thomas often dreamed about Lisa. Sometimes the vision of her was so real he would reach out for her, even call her name. Other times he saw the range and the longhorns moving across. Seldom did he dream about his wife or father, though when he did, one or the other was always pointing an accusing finger at him.

But not a night passed that some fragment of the war did not come full blown into his brain, forcing him to relive the violence of skirmish, the wild surge of a charge, the fury of battle. The shrieks of wounded men, the cries of stricken horses, the sharp crackle of rifle fire, the thunderous booming of cannon, even the acrid smell of burnt powder rose from his memory with startling clarity.

These things he had ingested. They were forever a part of him, a kind of vomit peculiar to men who survive battles.

Just before sunrise Thomas awoke with a start. But it was not a dream that wrenched him to full wakefulness. It was the low, dull rumble of thunder. He rubbed his eyes, and at the same time strained to catch the sound again.

Other men had heard it too and were awake, listening for the next rumble.

The boom came from the northeast, from the direction of the Chickahominy River.

Thomas scrambled to his feet. The three other company lieutenants clustered around him.

'Didn't you have your troop on patrol out that way?' Lieutenant Yancy asked, looking at Thomas.

'Not that far east,' he explained. 'We went as far as the Twin Pines, then swung west.'

'Too late in the season for a thunderstorm,' another officer said.

'There's the captain!' Thomas exclaimed.

Grayson came up to the men. 'What do you make of it?' he asked.

'Doesn't sound like our guns,' Thomas said.

The thundering was continuous and the predawn darkness in the northeast was rent by the intermittent white flashes of light.

'Why the hell don't our guns open up?' questioned Lieutenant Yancy.

'Maybe,' Thomas responded, 'we don't have any there.'

'And just what the hell does that mean?' Yancy challenged. 'If the damn Yankees have guns, you can bet your bottom dollar so do we.'

Thomas shrugged. Yancy had only been with the company for two weeks. He had gone on a few patrols and had fought in one skirmish. Thomas knew the man had not really been blooded. It would have been a waste of time to try to explain that the Confederate forces were sadly lacking artillery. Yancy would soon find that out for himself.

The whole company was up and every man had his face turned in the direction of the firing.

Suddenly the cannonading stopped.

'Ain't that just like the damn Yankees!' exclaimed Yancy loudly. 'They probably started that ruckus just to wake us up.'

Thomas glanced at him. 'If you think that,' he said tightly, 'you're a damn fool.'

'What did you say?' Yancy asked.

'You heard me clear enough,' Thomas answered, turning away from the man.

Yancy reached out. Before any of the other officers could stop him he grabbed Thomas' right arm and spun him around. 'I demand an apology!' he exclaimed. 'The rest of the officers are my witnesses.'

Thomas' hand jerked up and hung over the butt of his gun. 'Don't ever do that again,' he said in a low voice.

'As an officer and a gentleman —'

'You're making a fool of yourself, Yancy,' Lieutenant White told him.

'I do not have to take that kind of talk from Carey —'

Grayson stepped in front of Yancy. 'The enemy,' the captain said, 'in case you have forgotten, sits on the other side of the Chickahominy.'

'With all due respects to the captain,' Yancy said, 'I find that I must demand satisfaction from Lieutenant Carey.'

'You, sir,' Grayson answered, 'are in no position to demand anything of the sort. This is not a gentleman's gaming club, and though you may be an officer and a gentleman, you are first and last a soldier in the Confederate Army. Have I made myself clear?'

'Yes, sir!' Yancy exclaimed, coming to attention.

Grayson turned to Thomas. 'And you, sir would do well to curb your temper,' he said glancing down at Thomas' right hand. 'Now I suggest that since you are both brothers-in-arms, you shake hands and let this matter end here and now.'

Thomas knew that the captain's suggestion was in fact an order. He stepped forward and offered his hand.

'I accept your apology, Lieutenant Carey,' Yancy said and, without offering his hand, turned and walked away.

Both Thomas and Grayson were too surprised to speak. They looked questioningly at each other, smiled, and then started to laugh.

'Were we ever so young and trusting?' Grayson asked.

'I think I was older by several years when I was his age,' Thomas answered with a laugh.

The captain and Thomas started to walk toward the command tent, while the remaining two officers looked at each other and shook their heads with disbelief. When they were halfway to the tent Grayson stopped and said, 'We'll probably be ordered into action if the Yankees are on the move.'

'I expect so,' Thomas answered.

'Keep an eye on Yancy,' Grayson told him. 'If he lives, he might make a good officer.

'Maybe, and then again maybe not,' Thomas said. 'Like you told me yesterday, an officer has to be able to do more than fight. Men like Yancey hardly ever do that.'

Grayson nodded and said, 'I hope you're wrong … for his sake, and for the sake of his men.'

'I'll watch him,' Thomas said, 'but I'm not going to play nursemaid to him.'

'Fair enough,' Grayson answered. Then he looked down at the black, wet earth. 'I didn't know you and Sergeant Whipple were friends,' he said, looking up at Thomas. 'I'm sorry I went at you so hard.'

Thomas shook his head. 'Maybe I should have put the scouts out sooner,' he conceded, realizing he was giving up the opportunity to explain the conclusions he had reached about Whipple's death.

Grayson shrugged. 'From what some of the other men said, it wouldn't have made much difference.'

Thomas glanced around. 'Sun's up, but you'd hardly know it with the rain.'

Grayson nodded. 'Better see that the men are ready to move as soon as the order comes down from Regiment.'

'Yes, sir!'

Grayson smiled. The two men saluted each other and Thomas returned to his lean-to.

FOURTEEN

By early afternoon the rain had stopped, and a short while later the sun burned away a thin layer of clouds. For the first time in a week, the sky was blue.

Thomas sat in front of his lean-to, enjoying the touch of the sun's warmth on his face. He had spent the previous few hours readying his men for the action that was sure to come if the Yankees had crossed to the south side of the Chickahominy. At intervals throughout the day the sound of cannonading trembled through the air. Mostly it was Yankee artillery, but now and then the Confederate side fired back.

Earlier Thomas had seen ten riders enter the bivouac area and except to remind him that replacements were due to arrive, he paid little attention to the activity in front of the command tent, where new troopers were waiting for the captain. Thomas was much more concerned with the troopers under his command, that each of them had a full supply of ammunition, adequate rations for at least two days, and a full canteen of water.

As he thought about this, Thomas noticed that the ten riders in front of the command tent disbanded and by twos and threes set off to the different parts of the bivouac area where the various troops of the company were located. He realized that none of the riders were headed in the direction of his troop. Then he saw a lone man, leading his mount across the bivouac area. The trooper was coming directly toward him.

Thomas got to his feet. There was something familiar about the man, something about his walk and his tall, sparse body, and then he got a good look at the man's face. It was Herrick.

Thomas stood still. His heart started to race and his hand moved over his gun.

Herrick stopped some two paces in front of Thomas. 'I was told I'd find you here,' he said.

Thomas remained silent. Herrick's face still bore the scars of the whipping he had given him.

'You don't seem pleased to see me,' Herrick said with a thin smile on his lips.

'I should have thought,' Thomas answered, 'that a sergeant would know the proper way to report.'

Instantly Herrick stiffened to attention and said, 'Sergeant Bill Herrick reporting for duty as ordered, sir.' And he saluted.

Thomas returned the salute. Then he said, 'Stand at ease.' He paused for a moment and wondered what fate had thrown the two of them together again. 'I think we best get off on the right foot,' he told him. 'If you have anything to say, say it now. If it suits your purpose to be transferred to another troop, I will talk to the captain —'

'With the lieutenant's permission,' Herrick answered, 'I have no reason to request a change unless the lieutenant prefers to ask for my transfer for his own reasons.'

'I need a sergeant,' Thomas answered stiffly. 'Mine was killed yesterday on the way in from a patrol.'

'The captain told me that,' Herrick said.

Thomas took a deep breath and slowly exhaled. 'How long have you been in the army?' he asked.

'I enlisted as soon as the war started.'

'Any action?'

'Bull Run,' Herrick said. 'Oak Hills, Cheat Mountain — should I name them all?'

'No need to,' Thomas answered. 'The captain seems to think that we'll be going into action soon.'

'He told us that,' Herrick replied. 'But that shouldn't fret you none.'

Thomas looked straight at him. 'It frets any man who has any sense,' he said.

'Maybe yes or maybe no. Some men fret about taking a herd across a wash. Then again, some men do what they have to do without fretting in the least about it.'

Herrick's words brought back the past. Thomas could feel the anger rise in him. Several times his hand moved over his gun, but each time Herrick's eyes spotted the movement, and though there was never any change in the expression on his face, there was a mocking laughter in his eyes.

'I heard that some of the boys from Paso Diablo are with you,' Herrick said.

'A few.'

'And the rest?'

'Dead.'

Herrick shook his head. 'Ever run into — what's his name? The brother of the man you gunned down.'

'You're making a mistake,' Thomas said sharply, 'if you think I'm going to have your personal feelings interfere with your duty.'

'And what about *your* personal feelings, lieutenant? How much are you going to let them get in the way of your duty? I'm qualified for the opening in your troop. I've had the experience.'

Thomas nodded. 'The troop is off to the right, by those birch trees. Corporal Downs will get you fixed up with whatever gear you need. But let me warn you, I won't put up with any slipshod nonsense. The first wrong move you make, sergeant, will be your last.'

Herrick nodded.

'Neither of us has to like the other,' Thomas said. 'But you'll do what you're told regardless of your feelings for me. Understand?'

'No questions, sir.'

'Is there anything else you want to say?' Thomas asked.

Herrick hesitated.

'Go on!' Thomas urged. 'I don't want anything left unsaid that might cause trouble later on.'

'It's about that man,' Herrick told him.

'What man?'

'The one I mentioned a while back.'

'Zeb?'

'That's him,' Herrick said with a laugh. 'I just couldn't remember his name… Well, I met up with him in Memphis. He stood me a few drinks, but he can't hold his whiskey too well.'

'What has that to do with me?' Thomas asked.

'I'm gettin' to that,' Herrick replied. 'Anyway, after a few drinks ol' Zeb told me a wild story about how he and two friends of his —'

'It was no wild story,' Thomas said tightly.

'But he said —'

'It was no wild story,' Thomas repeated.

'But he said that you didn't even go after him.'

'No,' Thomas said quietly. 'I didn't. They left Helen in a bad way…'

Herrick looked at him questioningly.

'Is that all, sergeant?'

'Yes, sir!' Herrick said and saluted.

Thomas returned the salute. A few moments later, he sat down and watched Herrick lead his mount toward the area where his troopers were located. He shook his head. Having Herrick as his sergeant wasn't going to be easy. The hard feelings between them were still there. Probably they would always be there. But to ask Grayson to reassign Herrick would mean giving the captain an explanation of what had happened on the drive, and later in the sporting house. Grayson was a God-fearing man, and Thomas was not about to let himself open for the same kind of criticism that he had gotten for so many years from his father. He made up his mind to make the best of what in his opinion was a bad deal.

He thrust his hands into his pockets, and in the right one touched the letter he had put there the previous day when he was too angry to read it. For any other man, a letter from home was something important, the kind of thing that would make him withdraw from the rest of the men and seek a few minutes of privacy. But Thomas had no such feelings. All his letters came from Helen. William never wrote, and what Helen usually wrote about hardly interested him at all. She always managed to fill several pages with small talk about Ethan, the ranch, William, and now and again about her father.

Thomas took the letter from his pocket and looked at it, trying to decide whether he should open it or wait until he was in a better mood. Once the company was ordered to move, the opportunity to read it might not come for several days and since he already had it in his hand, there was no reason that he could think of to postpone reading it.

Carefully he tore one end of the envelope open and withdrew the two folded sheets of paper from it. Helen always opened her letters the same way: *My Dear Husband.* She wrote as though there was some feeling of love between them. He wondered how she did it and why. He shook his head and moved his eyes to the rest of the letter.

Once again I take pen in hand to write to you in order that you may know what is happening here. The weather for this time of year has been unusually warm but William insists that the winter will be a hard one. He has reached this conclusion because of the thickness of the hair on the cattle. He claims that is always a sign that the winter will be colder and snowier than usual.

Ethan is now weaned and toddles after his grandfather like a puppy dog. The two of them have a wonderful relationship. I think it would make you proud to see how well the two manage to do things together. The other day William took the child out on the range with him. That was a sight to behold!

Most of the young men have gone off to the war and there are thousands of strays on the range. And though there is a great need for beef, there is also a severe lack of ranch hands.

Last Sunday my father came out to dinner. He told us that he has it on good authority that General Lee will soon attempt to push into the North. Maybe if he does then the war will be over and you will be able to come home. He said that the South can and must win if we hope to retain our heritage and our rights.

And now I come to the saddest part of this letter. Your father received word — I did not ask him how or from whom it came — that your brother John was taken prisoner and is now in Libby Prison in Richmond.

Thomas stopped. He did not even know that John had returned from England and joined the Union Army. He continued to read.

Though your father would like to know more about John's condition, he could not ask you to see your brother.

Therefore, I am taking it on myself to ask that you make some attempt to visit John and inform us about him. Libby Prison is for Union Officers. Your father did not tell me what rank John held but I guess it was at least as high as your own.

Once more Thomas stopped reading. That John was a prisoner deeply disturbed him. He knew enough about the prisoner-of-war camps to know that conditions in them were less than tolerable. The food was bad, the discipline harsh, and the lack of sanitary facilities made even the best of them a place of pestilence.

He looked down at the rest of the letter.

We have not heard from Clem for several weeks. But we pray to God that he is safe. In his last letter he told us that his unit was reassigned to General Jackson's Army in the Shenandoah Valley.

I close now with love in my heart and a prayer on my lips that God see you safely back to us.

Your loving wife
Helen

Thomas slowly folded the letter, then a moment later unfolded it again and re-read what Helen had written about John. That his father could not bring himself to write about John infuriated Thomas to the extent that he silently cursed the old man. If only to find out what had happened between his father and John, Thomas vowed that he would go to Libby Prison to see his oldest brother.

So intense were his emotions that he failed to notice the shadow of the man standing in front of him.

'Excuse me, lieutenant,' the man said.

Thomas looked up and saw Herrick. 'Yes, sergeant, what is it?' The anger in him colored the tone of his voice.

Herrick was not prepared for the sharp response. He stepped back.

'You have something to say, sergeant?' Thomas asked, getting to his feet.

'It will keep,' Herrick answered.

'Suit yourself,' Thomas told him. 'But in the future, if you have something to tell me I expect to be told.'

'Yes, sir,' Herrick answered. He saluted and, turning around, started back to the troop.

'Sergeant?' Thomas called.

Herrick stopped and faced his commanding officer.

'There is no need to salute me —'

'I salute the uniform, not the man,' Herrick answered.

Thomas felt his cheeks burn. 'We are less formal here,' he said, 'than in some other units. Just do your job and keep as many men alive as you can and that will be more than enough.'

'Yes, sir!'

'Do you still feel that what you came to tell me can wait for another time?'

Herrick took a few moments to think before he answered. 'I just wanted to tell you,' he said, 'that maybe it would be better if I could be transferred to another troop.'

Thomas nodded. He understood how hard it was for Herrick to say that. 'We'll be going into action soon,' he answered. 'Let's see how it works out. Maybe I won't make it, then there'll be no need for you to transfer.'

'Could happen to me,' Herrick said.

Thomas nodded. 'That's why I think we should wait,' he said. 'But if you are set on transferring —'

'I'll wait.'

'What made you change your mind? I mean about asking to be transferred to another unit?'

He gestured helplessly. 'The men,' he answered. 'When I saw them I knew that I owed them more than what I could give them.'

'Because of me?'

Herrick nodded.

'At least you're honest about it,' Thomas said. 'What happens during the next few days will tell, won't it?'

'Yes.'

Thomas nodded and told Herrick to go back to the troop.

The night bloomed out of a fiery sunset and the deep-throated sound of cannonading to the northeast. A gentle warmth, more suited to a May night than one in October, lay over the land, and the moonless sky was filled with the scintillating light of stars too numerous to count.

The men in the bivouac were hardly conscious of the night's splendor. They stayed close to their mounts, expecting to hear the shrill bugle call of 'Boots and Saddles', but the anxious hours of waiting continued long past midnight and then most of the men turned in, having decided the fighting they had expected to do would have to be done on the morrow.

Thomas was more restive than usual. The incidents of the day that started with his row with Yancy and ended with his finding out that John was in Libby Prison seemed to indicate that something even more disastrous was in the offing. And, of course, the assignment of Herrick to his troop caused him concern.

Several times he dozed off, only to wake with a sudden start because he felt the presence of danger. But after a while he slept and began to dream.

Out of his memory rose, like the dead will rise from their graves on Judgement Day, the incident that had taken place between him and Herrick in the sporting house. He saw himself on the floor and felt the cut of the whip each time Herrick struck out at him, and then he saw himself in possession of the whip, returning in kind and more to Herrick…

The dream changed. He was back in the front room at the ranch watching Zeb cut and brand Helen. He was filled with the sense that just outside in the front yard there was something even more terrible than what was happening in front of him. He felt it! He could almost see it, although he never took his eyes off Zeb…

The dream was beginning to fragment and dissolve, but the feeling of impending danger remained and grew more tangible. The darkness that hovered outside of the room filled his brain. It seemed to hover over him. It was there!

Suddenly something struck his chest.

In an instant Thomas was awake. His hand went to his chest and his fingers closed around the twisting, writhing body of a snake. He held tight, and as he scrambled to his feet Thomas saw a shadow dart through the trees, toward where his troops were camped. He threw the snake to the ground with all the force he could muster, stunning the reptile just long enough for him to draw his saber and hack off its head.

Too furious to stop and think, Thomas impaled the still-writhing body on the point of his saber and ran to where his troopers were. He was determined to have done with Herrick once and for all, even if it meant killing him.

'Herrick!' Thomas shouted, entering the area where his men were. 'Sergeant Herrick!'

The troopers leaped to their feet.

Thomas was sweating profusely and breathing hard when he finally stopped in front of the fire. 'Sergeant Herrick,' he yelled. 'Goddam you, get your ass over here.'

Corporal Downs came forward. 'Are we going to move out?' he asked.

'I want Herrick,' he answered, waving the impaled snake in front of him.

'The sergeant is not in his blanket,' one of the troopers said.

Thomas took a deep breath. 'That was the last place I expected he would be,' he said. 'Now will one of you find him?'

'There's no need to do that,' Herrick answered, pushing his way through the knot of men around the lieutenant.

The instant Thomas saw him he thrust the limp remains of the snake at him. 'Was this the way, Herrick,' he snarled. 'The first time you used a whip, now this?'

The troopers drew back and formed a wide circle around their lieutenant and sergeant.

'I don't know what the hell you're talking about,' Herrick answered, pulling his suspenders on to his shoulders. He looked at the headless snake, but before he could ask about it Thomas demanded to know where he had been. 'In the latrine,' he answered.

'Then how did this drop on me?' Thomas asked, waving the saber at him.

'Crawled, I suspect,' Herrick answered calmly.

'You can do better than that,' Thomas challenged.

'Dropped from a tree?'

'That's much better, Herrick, much better,' Thomas told him. 'Except that I was not sleeping under any trees. But let me tell you how, sergeant. It was thrown on to my chest.'

Herrick started.

'But you know that, don't you?'

Herrick shook his head. 'I went to take a crap,' he said. 'I just told you that.'

'Who saw you?' Thomas shouted. 'Who saw you?'

Herrick remained silent.

'No one?' Thomas said tightly. 'No one saw you, because you didn't go to the latrine. You came up through the woods behind me and threw this snake on my chest!'

'You're daft!'

'What did you say, sergeant?' Thomas shouted.

'You're daft!' Herrick repeated.

A gasp of disbelief arose from the circle of men.

'First you try to kill me, then you're cocky enough to be insubordinate!' Thomas told him.

'Let's cut this shit out about you being a lieutenant and me a sergeant,' Herrick said, breathing hard. 'You need something to get rid of me once and for all, don't you?'

Thomas didn't answer.

'If you weren't so eager to accuse me of trying to kill you, you would have taken a good look at that snake.' He reached out and took hold of it. 'That's no damn viper,' he said mockingly. 'That's just a big old black snake.' And wrenching the lifeless length from the point of the saber, he held it close to the light of the fire for everyone there to see.

'Then who —'

'I don't know who,' Herrick said. 'And I don't know why. Maybe somebody was tryin' to play a practical joke. I said I was in the latrine taking a crap and that was where I was. I don't give a damn if you believe it or not.' He took a deep breath and said, 'And to think I was going to tell you how sorry I was about what happened to your wife — not that I ain't sorry for her — but you got what was coming to you. You keep looking for trouble, don't you? Well, this time you came to the wrong place for the wrong reason and to the wrong man.'

Thomas slowly lowered his saber.

'Maybe being a soldier is too much for you,' Herrick said. 'You like to do your killin' one at a time, man to man.'

'That's enough!' Thomas said tightly.

'Even if I did drop a snake on you,' Herrick said, 'you think I'd be fool enough to go against you with a gun? You're fast. There are damn few men who are faster. If I wanted to kill you I'd do it differently.' He jiggled the bloody body of the snake in front of him. 'I don't give a damn about you. I didn't come to this unit. I was ordered here. And I'm not in the army to settle a score with you. I joined up to fight Yankees.'

Thomas looked at the circle of men and knew that he had made a fool of himself in front of them. The times he had led them in battle counted for naught. He had wrongly accused one of their own of a hanging offense, and they had heard what Herrick had said about him. He was sure that the respect they felt for him no longer existed. Perhaps he should be the one to transfer to a different unit.

He started to walk away from the fire and the ring of men opened to let him pass. As soon as he was out of the area, Thomas quickened his step and went directly to his lean-to. He spent the rest of the night lying on his blanket roll, looking up into the deep reaches of the sky. Just before dawn, his eyelids became too heavy for him to hold open. They closed and Thomas slept.

FIFTEEN

During the next two days nothing happened, except that the cannonading from the Confederate side of the Chickahominy became more intense, and this served to lessen the tension of the men in the company.

The hardest part of any battle was always the time spent, by the men who would do the fighting, waiting for the actual conflict to begin. Thomas was more aware of this tension than he had been before any of the previous engagements in which he had fought. The time passed slowly and because of what had happened between him and Herrick he spent as little of it as possible with his men. What business he had with Herrick was taken care of with dispatch and in a completely formal manner. Neither he nor Herrick made any mention of the incident, and to his astonishment the entire matter never went beyond the men of his troop. Whether this was Herrick's doing or that of the men, who took it upon themselves not to discuss it with the other troopers of the company, Thomas was silently grateful to them for their willingness to protect his standing with the rest of the company.

But he was edgy and unable to free himself from the feeling that he was being watched by someone or something. He developed a bad case of the runs and did a lot of cigarette-smoking.

Late in the morning of the second day he wrote to Helen, telling her that he would go to Richmond to see John as soon as he could. Then he mentioned that he would probably be involved in a battle that seemed to be shaping up. He made no reference to his father or her and he wrote nothing about his son. When the letter was finished he reread it and, satisfied with what he had put down, signed his name.

He also wrote to Tiny, the barkeep at the Broken Horn, knowing that the man would read the letter to Lisa. Even as he wrote it, he desperately wanted to tell her how much he missed and loved her, but since she could neither read nor write, he would have been embarrassed to have Tiny read any tender sentiments to her. But he did send his regards to her and wish her well.

Though his actual written letters were brief, Thomas often composed long letters to Lisa, especially while riding. The longer he was separated from her, the more he realized how much he loved her.

Now when everything seemed to have gone wrong, his yearning for Lisa increased to the degree that made him wish he had never gone off to join the army, especially since the longer he was away, the more he realized that he did not hold with the cause of the Confederacy, either on the issue of slavery or the right of secession. His reason for being in the war was childishly simple. It gave him the excuse he needed to leave Helen, his father, and the ranch. At best that excuse grew weaker and weaker with each passing day. But there was little he could do about it. If he survived the war, he intended to go back to the ranch and tell his father that he was his own man, that even if it meant losing the ranch, he was going to divorce Helen and marry Lisa. That's what he would tell the old man, regardless of the consequences. The war had taught Thomas the value of living his life in a manner of his own choosing.

He signed the letter to Tiny, folded the single sheet of paper, and inserted it into an envelope which he had previously addressed. Then he walked across the bivouac area to put his two letters in the mail pouch that hung outside the command tent.

The threat of imminent battle finally came, but not in the way, or from the quarter, that the men in Thomas' company had expected it would. The intentions of the enemy were no easier to define than the direction of the wind when it blew in fits and starts from every direction of the compass.

The heavy Union shelling of the Confederate lines south of the Chickahominy proved to be nothing more than a feint, and while the men in Thomas' company and those of units close by looked toward the northeast for the next bloody contest, several squadrons of Yankee Cavalry crossed the Chickahominy to the west. Then circling behind the Confederate units, the blue-bellies destroyed them and swept east.

News of what had happened reached Captain Grayson by courier from Brigade headquarters, and with it came the simple order to hold — and if possible beat back — the enemy forces. But because the Yankees were moving so swiftly, Brigade was only able to supply sketchy information about the position of the enemy, which meant that Grayson's troopers would have to find as well as fight the Union forces.

The clear, brazen sound of 'Boots and Saddles' broke over the quiet of the bivouac area. The men responded instantly. Fires were quickly doused, mounts were saddled, and each of the four troops assembled in the center of the camp site.

Grayson summoned the officers to his tent and gave them a brief summary of the information he had received from Brigade. Then he read the orders he had received and told them they would have to find the battle first, since no one in Brigade knew where it was. He turned to the map laid out on his desk and said, 'The Chickahominy bows some fifteen miles upstream from where we are. The water at this time of the year is shallow enough for horses to ford.'

The officers peered down at the map.

'If they circled around to the south,' Lieutenant White said, 'they might not be too far away from us by now.'

'That's what I was thinking,' Grayson said. 'The road closest to where we are is this one here.' His finger moved along a thin red line. 'Iron Neck Road. I think they'll try to make the best use of that road to move farther east.'

'Why wouldn't they use the woods?' Yancy asked.

'The woods are all right for a patrol, but a large force would have trouble. It would slow them down too much. I think they'll use the road for the main body and guard their flanks with a troop or two.'

'How many men do you think they have?' Thomas asked.

'Two, possibly more, squadrons,' Grayson said.

'That's three times our number.'

Grayson smiled. 'There is a rumor about that any one of our men can whip a half dozen of theirs. Well, we only have to prove that we can beat half that number. Any other questions?'

'None,' the officers answered.

Grayson nodded. 'Lieutenant Yancy and his troop will ride under the command of Lieutenant Carey. The other two officers and their men will ride with me. Lieutenant Yancy, you look as though you want to say something.'

'If it is all the same to you, captain, I would prefer —'

'I don't give a damn what you would or would not prefer, lieutenant,' Grayson said sharply. His face became livid and his eyes narrowed down to slits. 'Up until now I have been patient with you, probably more patient than I should have been. Lieutenant Carey is not only senior to you in rank, but his experience does not come from a few patrols and one or two skirmishes. You will ride with him, lieutenant — and what is more, if I learn that you failed to follow his orders, I will personally see that you are court-martialed. Have I made myself absolutely clear?'

'Yes, sir,' Yancy answered, his cheeks so red that they looked as if they had just been slapped.

'Thomas,' Grayson said, addressing him by his given name for the first time.

Startled, Thomas looked up, but Grayson's attention was focused on the map.

'I want you to take the two troops out toward this area to the south and west of us about seven miles. There's a small hill that overlooks the terrain to the south and north. You'll have a good view of the road. Try to make them come after you. You'll have a better chance if you can do that.' Grayson finally raised his eyes.

'Yes, sir,' Thomas answered.

'I will try,' Grayson explained, 'to get the rest of the company around to their rear. With any luck we might be able to cut them up enough to make them drop back. Good luck, gentlemen, and may God bless you.'

Thomas waited until Grayson moved his men out. Then he raised his arm and slowly lowering it shouted, 'By a column of twos, forward, ho!' The order was repeated many times down the long line of mounted men.

A few minutes after the troopers cleared the bivouac area, a lone rider emerged from the woods and followed behind the column, though not too close, lest one of the troopers at the tail end of the column suddenly take a notion to look behind him.

The man did not want to be seen, not yet, and not by anyone else but Lieutenant Thomas Carey. He ran his hand over the grizzled stubble on his chin. He was damn annoyed that the company had moved out just when his little game had become interesting. Throwing the snake at Thomas was even better than killing the sergeant. Thomas took it so bad that he not only made a damn fool of himself but got a good case of the runs because of it. Just thinking about it made the man cackle with satisfaction. Then suddenly he brought himself up sharply. A rider was heading back down the road toward him. It was a trooper. He readied his gun, easing it slightly out of its holster.

'Hey, mister!' the trooper called, galloping up to the man and then reining his mount to a quick halt. 'Where the hell are ya goin'?'

'Jest yonder aways,' the man said, gesturing with his hand.

'Can't go thatta way,' the trooper told him. 'Goin' ta be some fightin' up thar pretty soon.'

The man made a clicking sound with his tongue.

'Best turn 'round an' find some other way,' the trooper said.

'Didn't know there was Yankees in an' aroun' dese parts,' the man said.

'Thar's a whole mess of 'em comin' thisa way too.'

'Much obliged,' the man said, touching the brim of his wide hat with a gesture that was almost a salute. 'You goin' ta fight?'

'Some, I guess.'

'Give those damn Yankees 'ell!'

'Sure'll try,' the trooper said.

The man knew that he was a scout, sent back to make sure that the blue-bellies weren't coming up behind the column. He also knew that when the trooper returned to the column he would report his presence. The man's right hand slipped down to the top of his boot.

'Trooper,' he said, 'tell t'e man in charge that if'n I see any blue-bellies back t'at way I'll come ridin' up an' tell ya.'

The trooper laughed. 'Mighty nice to know —'

The man's hand jumped up and a Bowie knife flew out of it.

The trooper gasped and dropped forward with three inches of steel in his chest.

The man grabbed the reins of the trooper's mount and led it into the woods, where he tethered it to a tree. Then he reached over and pulled his knife from the dead man's chest, letting the body fall to the ground. He wiped the blade clean of blood by rubbing the steel several times over his trousers. Then he put it back into his boot, wheeled his mount back on to the road and resumed following behind the column.

By the time Thomas' column reached the vicinity of the knoll, it was late in the afternoon and the weather that had held for two whole days was beginning to change. Already the sky was filled with leaden gray clouds that moved toward each other like huge ships of the line seeking to engage an unseen enemy. With the massing of the cloud, the light and warmth of the sun vanished. The wind picked up, shaking the multi-colored leaves on the trees so violently that many were torn from the more exposed branches and whirled across the road under the hooves of the horses.

Thomas halted the column about a half mile from the knoll. 'Sergeant Herrick?' he called.

'Yes, sir,' Herrick answered, wheeling out of his position some yards behind Thomas and galloping up to him.

'We'll wait here until our scouts return,' Thomas said. 'Pass the word for the men to rest easy.'

Lieutenant Yancy came riding up. 'Anything wrong?' he asked.

'No,' Thomas answered.

'Then why have we stopped?'

'For the scouts to report back.'

Yancy glared at him, swung his mount around and galloped back to his own troop.

'Will that be all, sir?' Herrick asked.

Thomas nodded.

'Would the lieutenant mind,' Herrick asked, 'if the men dismounted while we waited?'

'No,' Thomas replied.

Herrick eased his horse back and then returned to the column.

Thomas studied the knoll. Topographically it was different from the way it had appeared on the map. There it was shown to be an elongated hill with a constant altitude along its top. But it was really saddle-shaped, with its eastern end considerably higher than the highest point on its western side. Its northern slope was steep and at its base the woods angled out sharply toward the road. In the event that the column had to fall back, the woods would offer the best protection unless the enemy cut them off.

A sudden gust of wind chilled him and, raising his broad collar to protect himself from the cold, Thomas waited impatiently for the scouts to return.

Thomas glanced up at the sky. It was completely covered with dark-gray clouds. He lowered his eyes and looked toward the knoll again. He could not shake the feeling that he was being watched. It clung to him like some slimy film that he could not wash away.

The sound of a rider coming up behind him brought Thomas out of his own brooding. He turned and saw Yancy.

'That trooper I sent back has not returned yet,' the young officer said, reining up.

'How long has he been gone?' Thomas asked.

'Better than an hour.'

'Send two more men back,' Thomas told him, 'but tell them to hurry. I don't want to have Yankees behind me as well as in front of me.'

'How could those blue-bellies have gotten to our rear?'

Thomas would have enjoyed giving Yancy some sort of flippant, ridiculous answer, but instead he shrugged and said, 'If they're there we'll have more than enough to worry about without trying to figure out how they managed to get there.'

Yancy gave him a peculiar look, but said nothing, and galloped back to his own troop.

A few minutes later the scouts returned. They reported that the knoll was safe and that there were no signs of the Yankee force anywhere nearby.

Thomas told them to re-join the column and then gave the order for the troopers to mount up. The column began to move again and continued until it reached the northern slope of the knoll.

'Not much room to move around up here,' Herrick commented.

Thomas agreed. 'But it does give a good clear view of the surrounding countryside,' he said.

'Won't do us much good if it starts to rain.'

'Neither will it do the Yankees much good,' Thomas answered. 'If we can't see them, they sure as hell will have trouble seeing us.'

'You think we'll be able to hold them?'

'For a little while,' Thomas replied. 'But not a helluva lot longer than that.'

'What about the other troops with the captain?'

'I guess they'll give us as much support as possible. Better signal the column to move on up.'

Herrick moved back to the other side of the saddle, took off his hat and began waving it. 'They're coming,' he called out.

Yancy was the first one up and he rode over to Thomas. 'Have you decided where you want my men?' he asked.

Thomas thought for a moment, then he said, 'In reserve. I want them held in reserve.'

Yancy paled. His lips trembled. Finally he said, 'With all due respects to your judgement, sir, I think we would be able to give a better account of ourselves if we struck at the enemy with both troops.'

Thomas took a deep breath and slowly exhaled. 'Our purpose, lieutenant, is to hold them — maybe, with some luck, turn them back. We are not here to give a good account of ourselves. You will hold your troop at the base of the knoll. If the Yankees attempt to circle round to our rear, you and your men will try to give us enough time to pull back and get to the woods. Is that understood?'

Yancy nodded.

Thomas looked around him. 'I don't expect that we'll be able to hold this knoll for long,' he said, more to himself than to Herrick or Yancy. 'But if the Yankees take it they'll have to pay a price. Maybe they won't want to pay so much for something that's as worthless as this knoll is. All right, lieutenant, get your men into position.'

'Yes, sir!' Yancy answered sharply, and immediately wheeled around.

'He's mighty anxious to fight,' Herrick said, as soon as Yancy was out of earshot.

'Before this is over,' Thomas replied, 'he might change his mind.' Then he told Herrick where to position the men from his troop. A third of the men were placed along the midsection of the knoll. Several of the remaining men were placed on the two high points, giving them the task of protecting the flanks of men in the center. With Corporal Downs in charge, the rest of the troop drew off to the far right and took up their position at the base of the knoll to prevent the enemy from flanking it on that side.

Thomas had several of the troopers fell some trees, which were then stripped of their branches and dragged up to the center of the knoll where they were set down to form a crude breastwork for the men. Everything was ready, and once more the waiting began.

Yancy came back up to the saddle of the knoll; with him were two troopers. 'Lieutenant,' he explained, 'these are the two men I sent back to look for the first man.'

'Did you find him?' Thomas asked.

'Sure did,' one of the troopers answered. 'He was dead.'

'Looked like a knife wound,' the second man added. 'His horse was tethered to a tree 'bout twenty feet from the road.'

'Any signs of the Yankees?' Thomas questioned.

'Nary a one,' the first trooper said. 'But we did see some guy jest ridin' along, and we tol' 'im to get the 'ell off the road.'

'We asked him if he saw anyone,' the other man said. 'But he said he didn't.'

'Was he on the road when you came back?' Thomas answered.

'No, sir,' the first man answered. ''E must 'ave scaddled into de woods.'

'What the hell was a civilian doing back there?' Yancy asked.

'I don't know,' Thomas answered.

'Sir,' one of the troopers said, 'I don't think he was from aroun' here.'

'Why?' Yancy asked.

The trooper looked at Thomas. 'He wore his gun low, the way Lieutenant Carey does — like most men from Texas. An' his hat was western style too, so were his boots.'

'There was a Sharp's rifle in 'is saddle 'olster,' the other men added.

For the first time since it happened, Thomas remembered the sound of shot that had killed Whipple. He knew then that it had been from a Sharp's rifle, but he had put it out of his mind almost as quickly as he had realized it.

'Did you get a good look at the man?' Thomas asked in a low voice.

'Not much to see,' the trooper who spotted the Sharp's rifle answered. 'His face was covered with a beard, but he looked like 'e knew 'ow to use t'at gun 'e was wearin'. '

Thomas nodded and thanked the troopers.

After Yancy had ordered his men back to the troop he again asked Thomas what a civilian was doing in the area.

'Just be glad he isn't a Yankee,' Thomas answered.

'We don't know that for sure.'

Thomas glanced at Herrick. 'You think he might be a Yankee?'

'Not from the way he was rigged out,' Herrick responded.

'Well, who the hell is he?'

'These woods are full of people —' Herrick started to say.

'I don't like it,' Yancy said. 'I have one dead trooper and there's some strange man out there. I tell you, lieutenant —'

'Return to your troop, lieutenant,' Thomas ordered, 'and I mean instantly!'

Yancy spurred his mount and the animal went charging down the slope.

Thomas looked at Herrick and said, 'I don't like it either.'

'You don't think that man is a Yankee, do you?' Herrick asked.

Thomas shook his head. 'But I sure as hell would like to know who he is, and why he is here. We're a long way from Texas. And if those troopers were right, the man they saw came from Texas.'

Herrick nodded but said nothing.

'Well,' Thomas commented, 'one man in the woods behind us is nowhere as bad as having a squad or two of Yankee cavalry there, now is it?'

'I'd feel better if no one was there,' Herrick answered.

'You're beginning to sound like Yancy,' Thomas chided.

For a moment the two men looked at each other.

Herrick smiled.

Thomas began to chuckle.

And they both began to laugh. But their mirth was short-lived as Yankee scouts came into view.

'Pass the word to the men,' Thomas said. 'I want every damn shot to count, and I don't want any shooting until I give the order.'

Herrick nodded and, stooping over, he scurried below the level of the knoll to carry out his mission.

Thomas had one of the troopers run down to Yancy and tell him that the enemy force was in sight. He sent another trooper to Corporal Downs with the same message.

The two Yankee scouts came within fifty yards of the knoll and then one rode back to the main body while the other dismounted to stretch and rest his horse.

Herrick re-joined Thomas just as the first rank of the enemy column came into view. 'How many do you think there are?' he asked.

'Three, maybe four, times our number,' Thomas answered, trying to keep his mouth moist by forcing saliva into it.

Several more minutes passed.

The front rank of the advancing column was within rifle range of Thomas' troopers. 'Ready, men!' he called out in a voice just loud enough for the men closest to him to hear.

'Ready,' the men answered one by one.

'Just a little closer,' Thomas said aloud, though he was really talking to himself. A moment passed and then another and a third —

'Fire!' Thomas shouted. 'Fire!'

In an instant a fusillade of deadly fire erupted from the knoll.

A man screamed. The first rank of the enemy column fell. Several riderless horses raced down the road. The second went down and so did the fourth. The air was filled with smoke and the smell of powder. What was left of the leading platoon raced off to the right, while the other units broke out of the line of march and reformed, keeping well out of the range of the rifles on the knoll.

'They'll be on us now!' Herrick exclaimed.

'Make your shot count!' Thomas exhorted his men. 'Here they come!'

Four squads of Union cavalry came pounding toward them. The beating hooves sounded like the throb of drums that grew louder and louder with each passing moment. The ground began to tremble. Their outstretched sabers flashed in the grayness of the twilight. They were close enough for their shouting to rise above the constant throb of the galloping horses.

Enough of them were charging toward the knoll to overwhelm Thomas' position. If Grayson was going to make his move, he should make it in the next few seconds, or —

Herrick tapped him on the shoulder and pointed off to the left.

'Good God!' Thomas exclaimed when he saw what was happening. Yancy had moved his troop out from behind the knoll and was now leading them against the left flank of the on-charging Union Force.

'It's not going to work,' Thomas said. 'As soon as they recover from his strike, they'll cut him down.'

'Something is happening out there,' Herrick said, pointing out into the distance.

'Grayson!' Thomas shouted. 'Grayson hit their rear!' He suddenly realized that other Yankee units would swing around his unguarded left flank and come up his rear. 'Let's get the hell out of here.'

Just at that moment Yancy's troopers slammed against the flank of the oncoming Union force. The charge was instantly broken. Yancy's men slashed and hacked their way into the ranks of the enemy force. The men screamed and killed each other in a frenzy of movement.

'Order the men down to their horses,' Thomas said. 'We'll join Corporal Downs and maybe draw enough blood to make those bastards fall back.'

Minutes later Thomas' troop was completely assembled. As soon as the troop was on the other side of the knoll, they formed two long lines.

'Draw sabers,' Thomas shouted. 'Trot … gallop … charge!'

The last word was taken up by the other men as they rushed toward the main body of the Union Cavalry.

Thomas crouched low in the saddle, his right hand holding the saber just off to the side of his horse's ear. The men were shouting. He was shouting, yelling, screaming inarticulate cries of rage, of the lust for blood.

Suddenly a figure in a blue uniform swung into view. Thomas slashed at it. His saber crunched through bone. The figure bled underneath Thomas' horse.

A face came into focus and he drove the saber into it. The man screamed and grasped at the blood-drenched blade, trying to tear it out of him. But Thomas lifted his foot and drove it into the man's belly, knocking the trooper from the saddle and at the same time freeing his saber.

The flick of a shadow crossed his left eye. Thomas swung his saber and caught the downward thrust of a Union trooper's blade against the naked steel of his own. The force of the blow shivered along the length of his arm, driving his arm down and throwing him off balance. The trooper's blade came at him again, but one of Thomas' men saw what was happening and threw himself on the blue-belly. The two men tumbled to the ground and Thomas wheeled away, driving his saber against the neck of the nearest foe, and as he drew back the blade, a curtain of blood came with it.

Thomas hacked his way through a blur of blue-jacketed, screaming men. The violence of the melee limited his reality to the man he was killing. Over and over again he heard himself shout, 'Kill the Yankee bastards! Kill them!' Then suddenly he felt the violent shock of a blade against his left arm. Instantly it was consumed with scorching pain. He wheeled and blindly struck out at his attacker, severing the man's hand with a single stroke.

Horses were rearing up, crying with terror as they were slashed by saber strokes meant for their riders. Wounded men were screaming in agony as they tried to escape from the hooves of the wild movements of the horses.

Some men were unsaddled and, dropping their sabers, used revolvers. Explosion after explosion added to the din of screams and shrieks and steel crashing against steel.

Thomas fought his way close to Herrick. 'Not many of us left,' he shouted.

'God help us!' Herrick called back.

The carnage swirled across the southern slope of the knoll, and from its highest point the man wearing a broad-brimmed hat and Texas boots watched the bloody contest with the relish of a sportsman. And though he could see the entire field, his eyes were fastened to Thomas Carey. Each time a Union trooper came close to killing Thomas, the man swore and cursed, shouting that Thomas Carey was his and his alone.

Suddenly the Yankee bugles rose above the din of battle and sounded recall. The men scurried down the far side of the knoll and dashed for the woods.

'They're falling back!' Thomas shouted. 'Men, they're falling back.' He brought his mount to a halt and looked about him. A dozen men were still in the saddle. The rest had been killed or wounded.

Herrick came up to him. 'Do we go after them?' he asked, pausing to gulp air into his lungs between each word.

'No,' Thomas answered.

'What about the captain?' Herrick questioned.

Thomas shook his head. 'Let's hope he got away,' he answered. He looked toward the base of the knoll. Bodies were strewn in every direction. Again he shook his head, and then ordered his men to make for the woods on the other side of the knoll as quickly as possible, afraid that the Union cavalry would try to attack again.

The men spurred their mounts to a gallop. As they swung around the right side of the knoll and came close to the woods, Thomas and Herrick were side by side. Then suddenly in the dim light Thomas saw the figure of a man. He was standing close to a large oak tree. A moment later he realized the man held a rifle.

'Herrick!' Thomas shouted.

But it was too late.

A single shot rang out. Herrick clutched at his chest and then tumbled from the saddle.

Thomas swerved off to the right, where he saw the man, but there was no one there. As he wheeled his mount around to go back for Herrick, Thomas knew with absolute certainty that someone was out to kill him but was making a game of it. He looked back at the oak. The time would come when they would face each other, and then…

The rain started just as Thomas dismounted and bent over Herrick. He looked up at the dark sky and whispered, 'I would have told him I was sorry about —' He stopped. It made little sense for Thomas to say what he would have done.

He lifted Herrick's body into his arms and carried it to where the other troopers stood, waiting in the cover of the woods.

SIXTEEN

It took Thomas several days to bring the remnants of his troop to Brigade Headquarters, where he related to Colonel Baxton, a man with gray hair and a cherubic face, what had happened to the company. The colonel listened to the story without interrupting, but as soon as Thomas had finished he said, 'Your attack turned the Yankees back, and when they reached the Chickahominy they were hit by several of our units. Not many of them crossed back to the other side of the river.'

'They fought bravely,' Thomas said.

The colonel nodded and said, 'So did your men.'

'Not only my troop,' Thomas explained. 'Captain Grayson struck at their rear —'

'Then you don't know about the captain?'

'Know what?'

'He was taken prisoner,' the colonel said. 'Those of his men who were not killed — well, I need not bother you with that. But for your outstanding performance, lieutenant, I am recommending that you be promoted to the rank of captain, and as soon as we reorganize, you will be given your own command.'

'Thank you, sir,' Thomas responded, sensing the colonel's attitude toward Grayson and the others who had surrendered.

'Have you been to see the surgeon about that wound?'

'Not yet.'

'Better tend to it as soon as you leave here.'

'Yes, sir,' Thomas said, and then he added, 'I request the colonel's permission for a five-day leave and ask the same privilege be granted to the men who returned with me.'

'Permission granted,' the colonel said without hesitation. Then he asked, 'But where will you go in so short a time?'

'To Richmond,' Thomas answered.

The colonel smiled. 'I know of several places where a man —'

'No, sir, but thank you anyway.'

'Then you have a lady there?'

Thomas shook his head. 'No, sir,' he answered. 'I want to see my brother.'

'What unit is he with?'

'None, sir.'

'I don't understand,' the colonel said.

'He's a prisoner-of-war,' Thomas answered, looking straight at his commanding officer. 'He's in Libby Prison.'

'That's the crime of this war,' the colonel said. 'Brother set against brother because of — I guess you know why.' Then he smiled and added, 'I'm glad you're on our side, very glad.' He stood up and reached across the desk to shake Thomas' hand. 'If you want to take a few more days in Richmond —'

'Five will be sufficient,' Thomas answered. He saluted and left the colonel's tent.

The next morning Thomas left for Richmond. Traveling with him were the men of what was left of his troop. He was happy to have them for company.

It took them a full day to reach the city and by the time they arrived it was too late for Thomas to see his brother, but it did give them time to do some drinking and whoring. They spent the night in a brothel and Thomas slept soundly at the side of a woman whose name he did not know when he embraced her, and whose name he would forget soon after he left the establishment.

Just before nine o'clock in the morning, Thomas waited in a small room for the guard to bring his brother John to him. There was one barred window through which the sun streamed. A table and two chairs were its only furnishings. Thomas guessed the room must be used for interrogation.

The walls were spotted with splotches of dried blood, around which some late-season flies clustered.

The door opened. Thomas turned toward it.

The guard pushed John into the room. His hands were bound. He was gaunt and his dark eyes were alive with fire.

'There's no need for that!' Thomas snapped.

John looked at him and his jaw went slack with surprise.

'He may be your brother, lieutenant,' the guard said, 'but he's my prisoner.'

'Thomas,' John whispered. 'My little brother Thomas!'

'I'll call you when I'm ready to leave,' Thomas told the guard.

'Sorry, lieutenant,' the man answered, 'the rules say —'

'Damn the rules!' Thomas shouted.

'Never mind the guard,' John told him. 'Don't waste your time arguing about whether he stays or goes. There's so much I want to know.'

Thomas suddenly found himself with his arms around John. 'I came as soon as I could,' he said. 'I would have been here, but my unit —'

'Let's not talk about the war,' John said. 'I want to know about you and the ranch.'

'I haven't been back there for a long time,' Thomas answered.

The two brothers sat down facing each other.

John smiled. 'Not nearly as long as I have been gone,' he said. 'Why, by God, the last time I saw you, you were ten, maybe twelve years old. And now look at you!'

'Clem told me you were in England,' Thomas said.

John nodded. 'How is he?' he asked.

'Alive and well, I hope,' Thomas answered. 'He's with General Jackson.'

'Have you heard from Pa?'

Thomas looked down. 'We don't write to each other,' he said.

'Then how do you keep in touch?'

'My wife —'

'You're married?' John exclaimed. 'That's wonderful!'

'It's not the way you think,' Thomas told him. 'I don't love her.'

'Then why did you marry?'

'Pa —'

'That meddling old fool!' John said harshly. 'Hasn't he learned to —' He stopped. 'I didn't mean to insult him,' he explained, 'but he just can't see the forest for the trees.'

'I know that,' Thomas answered with a smile. 'He sees only what he wants to see.' Then he looked straight at his brother. 'I think he still loves you, even though you've been away so long.'

John nodded. 'I know,' he said. 'He'd be a much better man if he'd let go of the past.'

'What really happened between the two of you?' Thomas asked.

'Didn't Pa ever tell you?'

Thomas shook his head.

'I found out his secret,' John said with a forced chuckle. 'I guess I was fourteen, maybe closer to fifteen when I went to his trunk and found something he had written.'

'A diary?'

'Something like that,' John answered. 'It was more an account of his life, at least the early part of it. I read it, and Pa found me reading it … that was when the trouble between us began. It lasted until I was your age, then I couldn't take it. I left and made my own way.'

'What was in it?'

John looked at the guard, shrugged and said, 'It seems that our grandfather sired a child by a woman other than his wife. When the woman died, he brought the child home and his legal wife raised it as her own. But somehow the child found out that he was a bastard and he almost killed his father — and, according to what Pa put down, drove the woman who had raised him to an early grave.'

'Pa wrote all that?' Thomas asked, shifting his position in the chair.

John nodded.

'You mean Pa never knew his real mother?'

'Not likely,' John told him.

'But you weren't much more than a boy when you found that out,' Thomas said, standing and walking to the window.

'I guess Pa felt that I had uncovered his nakedness, so to speak. And for that, in the true biblical sense, he could not forgive me. He had to cast me out and he did.'

Thomas shook his head and returned to the chair, but did not sit down. 'I don't understand —'

'He was afraid I would discover that his strength was really his weakness,' John said. 'You see, he's terrified of Grandfather Ethan's hot blood showing up in either him or any of us. He used to whip the daylights out of me and shout that I had the Carey blood in me … well, who the hell else's blood would I have?'

'To spite him,' Thomas said, 'I named my son Ethan.'

'You did what?' John asked, getting to his feet. Then suddenly he began to laugh. 'Oh, my God, that must have really gotten to him.'

Thomas nodded. 'He's a hard man,' he said.

'You don't look as though you're particularly easy,' John commented.

'I guess not,' Thomas responded. 'But if I wasn't hard, he would have chewed me up and spit me out any time he felt like it.'

'Time's up!' the guard said.

'I'll be here tomorrow,' Thomas told his brother.

'And so will I,' John laughed as the guard herded him out of the door.

Thomas was glad to be out of the prison. He glanced up at the sun. It was bright, and the sky around it was very blue. He couldn't imagine himself penned up in a place where he would never be able to look at the sun or the sky or inhale air that didn't stink of sweat and decay. No, he would not be able to endure it. He lowered his eyes, looked back at the prison walls and went to meet his men.

Thomas walked slowly, thinking about what John had told him. It didn't seem possible that William could have been so afraid of the 'Carey blood' as to have let his fear dominate him. That fear had reached out from Thomas' grandfather to him and John. Because of it, John had left the ranch and Thomas had been forced into a marriage he never wanted. Thomas realized how frightened his father must have been, to have taken such drastic actions to prevent 'the bad blood' from showing itself. Even the old man's intense religious devotion was suddenly open to question.

For the first time in his life, Thomas pitied his father and he saw him as John did. William was a foolish old man!

When it came time for Thomas to say goodbye to John at the end of his second visit, he was too choked up to speak and grasped his brother's hands.

'Tell Pa,' John said, 'that someday I'll come back.'

'I'll write and tell him,' Thomas answered, coughing to clear his throat.

'And take care of yourself, hear?' John told him.

'Yes.'

John started to go, then stopped. 'What I told you about Pa,' he said, 'you must not give him cause to guess that you know.'

'I won't.'

'If I don't make it,' John said, 'promise me that your next son will have my name?'

Thomas nodded.

'A man likes to know that he leaves something behind him,' John said with a small smile. And then the guard hustled him out of the room.

Thomas left the prison and went to the nearest saloon. He drank several whiskies before he re-joined his men.

The remainder of the day and a good part of the night was a blur. He and his men did a lot more drinking and spent the night in another brothel. But by morning they were saddled up for the long ride back to Brigade.

As soon as Thomas reported his return to the duty officer he was told that Colonel Baxton wanted to see him.

'About what?' Thomas asked.

'I don't rightly know,' the duty officer answered. 'But I wouldn't put off seein' him. The colonel can become mighty touchy about sech things.'

Thomas nodded and went straight to the Headquarters' tent.

The colonel welcomed him warmly and came straight to the point. 'Lieutenant,' he said, 'how would you feel about going on patrol again?'

'When?'

'Tonight,' the colonel replied. 'There's something going on on the other side of the Chickahominy, and we want to know about it before it's too late.'

'How many other men do I take?' Thomas asked.

'One,' the colonel answered. 'We want information, nothing more.'

Thomas nodded. 'How long do I have before I'm to report back?'

'The sooner the better,' the colonel replied. 'Get close enough to see what's happening and then get back here.'

'I'll take Corporal Downs with me,' Thomas said.

The colonel nodded, then stood up and went to the map that hung on the tent wall behind his desk. 'We're here,' he said, pointing to a position on the map. 'The Yankees are over here.' His finger moved to another spot. 'That's less than eight miles from where we are. If you're lucky you can make it there and back before sunup.'

'I'll try,' Thomas answered.

'Any questions?'

'Couldn't some other officer —'

'Most of them around Brigade are not field-trained,' Baxton said. 'Besides, you have the experience and would know what you were looking at.' Then he added, 'I know you won't do anything stupid.'

'Let's hope not,' Thomas replied with a smile. 'I'd like to draw a captain's pay.'

Baxton laughed and wished him luck.

Two hours later Thomas and Corporal Downs were on the south side of the Chickahominy. There was a heavy mist on the river and along its banks. Downs rode behind Thomas.

'Where're you fixin' to cross, lieutenant?' Downs asked in a low voice.

'Some place where we can see the other side,' Thomas answered. 'I would not want to run smack into a Yankee patrol.'

They moved upstream without further conversation.

The man who had watched the battle from the ridge of the knoll was following close behind the corporal.

He had watched Thomas leave the Brigade area some four days before and he had seen him return earlier that very night. And when Thomas and the corporal rode out on patrol, he knew the time had come for him to make his move.

The game was running too long, and he was afraid of losing the opportunity to earn the rest of the money due him for killing Thomas. Each time the lieutenant went out on patrol there was the possibility that some Yankee might do what he had been hired to do.

The man moved in closer, dropped his hand to the top of his right boot and withdrew the Bowie knife. He waited until the corporal's back was no more than ten feet in front of him before he threw the knife.

'Lieutenant —'

The blade struck Downs between the shoulders.

Thomas turned. He watched the corporal slide to the right and drop from the saddle. Just behind the unmounted horse he saw another rider.

Thomas' hand went to his gun. It came smoothly out of its holster.

'Fire it,' the man said, 'an' every Yankee aroun' 'ere'll come a-runnin'.'

The voice — Thomas knew the voice. He had heard it before. He started to dismount, but he had hesitated too long. A loop swung over him and he was wrenched from the saddle. The gun dropped from his hand as he tried to pull free.

'Won't 'elp ya none,' the man said, chuckling softly. 'I got ya 'og-tied. Now all I gotta do is gut ya an' truss ya up like a big ol' bird.'

'You're going to have to get close to me first,' Thomas said.

'Sure enough!' the man answered. 'But I got ya tied ta de 'orn of my saddle,' he said. 'I got me a good cow pony.'

Thomas was able to move his hands and his forearms, but from his shoulders to his elbows the rope held him. Rather than pull away on the rope and tighten it, he moved toward the man and to the right, where there were a few trees.

'Didn't figure it ta be so easy,' the man said.

'You haven't got me yet,' Thomas answered, still trying to place the voice.

The man was following the rope. Thomas could feel it vibrate as the man moved along it. He waited until the man was half a dozen feet from him and then he rushed him, smashing his body into the man's side and knocking him to the ground.

Using the movement available to him in his hands and forearms, Thomas twisted several loops of rope around the man's legs. He worked swiftly, and before the man could regain his breath, he had him tied. Then he rolled him over.

It was Zeb.

'It's not going to be so easy now!' Thomas hissed, filled with rage.

Zeb's hands flailed at him.

Thomas leaped free.

Zeb tried to get up, but found his legs were tied. He went for his gun.

Thomas kicked it out of his hand. 'You killed three men to get to me,' he told Zeb. 'Well, now you have me, but I have you too.'

Zeb grabbed hold of Thomas' foot and tried to bring him down, but Thomas drove his other one into Zeb's chest, crunching several of his ribs. Zeb groaned with pain.

'I got more than a score to settle with you,' Thomas told him as he watched him writhe. 'More of a score than killing you three times over would satisfy.' He slammed his boot into Zeb's side again. 'Who sent you to bushwhack me?' Thomas asked. 'Who sent you? I'd just as soon kick you to death as kill you any other way.'

Zeb rolled over. A moment later he jerked Thomas' foot out from under him. Zeb was on him. His hands closed around Thomas' throat and began to squeeze the life out of him.

Thomas fought to get free, then he suddenly remembered his knife, and struggled to reach it. Finally his fingers closed around the hilt. He jerked up and the blade came from its sheath. The next instant he cut the rope that bound him. As soon as his hands were free Thomas dropped the knife and then drove his fist against the side of Zeb's head, stunning him.

It took Thomas a moment to catch his breath, then he pushed free of Zeb.

'Who sent you?' Thomas croaked. His voice had a gravelly sound. Each word he spoke sent bolts of pain shooting through his throat.

'Don't make no difference now,' Zeb said, breathing hard.

'Makes a difference to me. Tell me and I'll get it over with fast —'

Zeb began to laugh. 'Ya don't know, do ya?'

'I didn't even know you were trying to kill me. I thought you would have had enough that night back at the ranch.'

Zeb was still laughing. 'It were Johnson —'

'He had no cause,' Thomas said. He was past being angry. He knew what he was going to do, but first he had to know who had sent Zeb. 'Johnson had no cause,' he said again.

Zeb stopped laughing. 'Your pa went to him,' he said. 'Johnson came to me and I came to you.'

'My pa?'

Zeb laughed. 'That's what's so funny,' he said. 'I ain't never kilt the son —'

Blinded with rage, Thomas lifted his foot and brought his rowled spur down on Zeb's neck. The man screamed and his body jerked up, blood gushing out of the wound.

'You lie!' Thomas shouted. 'You lie! He wouldn't do that to his own son.'

Zeb shook his head. 'God's own truth,' he said, blood gurgling from his mouth.

Thomas lifted his foot again and tore open more of Zeb's throat. 'Now tell me —'

'Your pa!' He laughed. 'Your pa!'

For the third time Thomas started to lift his foot when he suddenly felt the sharp jab of a rifle in his back.

'Easy, Reb,' a voice said. 'Just take it easy!' A moment later several Yankee soldiers were around Thomas.

'Good God!' one of the soldiers said, looking down at Zeb. 'The man's throat is torn open!'

'Let's get this one back across the river,' another said. 'Just keep your hands high above your head, lieutenant. We got us quite a walk to take.'

Thomas remained motionless. A red mist clouded his vision. His body still throbbed with anger and a tight feeling in his chest forced him to gulp air.

'Com' on, Reb,' the man urged, prodding his captive with the rifle. 'Move!'

Thomas began to walk. Slowly the red mist left his eyes and he realized what had happened. The enormity of what his father had done lay on his shoulders like a great weight and bent his back. Thomas had hated Zeb and had killed him … and someday he would return home and kill his father.

But even as Thomas made this vow, his throat tightened and he clenched his teeth to stifle a sob of despair…

A NOTE TO THE READER

Dear Reader,
If you have enjoyed the novel enough to leave a review on **Amazon** and **Goodreads**, then we would be truly grateful.
Sapere Books

Sapere Books is an exciting new publisher of brilliant fiction and popular history.

To find out more about our latest releases and our monthly bargain books visit our website: **saperebooks.com**

www.ingramcontent.com/pod-product-compliance
Lightning Source LLC
Chambersburg PA
CBHW051511030726
47592CB00006B/2214